Praise for Stephanie Bond

"*My Favorite Mistake* certainly illustrates the author's gift for weaving original, brilliant romance that readers find impossible to put down."
—*Wordweaving.com*

"Sassy, ultra-sexy."
—*Romantic Times BOOKclub on Cover Me*

"There should be a notice on her books:
For a really GOOD time, read Stephanie Bond!"
—*America Online Romance Fiction Forum*

"True-to-life, romantic and witty, as we've come to expect from Ms. Bond."
—*The Best Reviews*

"Stephanie Bond never fails to entertain me and deserves to be an auto-buy."
—*Romance Reviews Today*

A starred review! "DO read this novel."
—*Publishers Weekly on Kill the Competition*

"With its energetic prose and cozy Southern setting, this read is a sterling source of laughs and lighthearted fun."
—*Publishers Weekly on I Think I Love You*

"Bond's fun and frothy story keeps the plot twists coming."
—*Publishers Weekly on Our Husband*

Blaze™

Dear Reader,

Have you ever wanted to be fearless? Have you ever looked back on a situation and wished you'd taken a chance rather than played it safe? I have. And so has Gabrielle Flannery. When a humiliating incident at work makes her realize that she's in danger of fading into the wallpaper if she doesn't make a change, she finds inspiration—in a magazine article—to take a big risk with her life, unaware it will lead to taking an even bigger risk with her heart!

Personally, I've made a vow to be more adventurous, and I hope that after reading *Just Dare Me...*, you, too, will challenge yourself to try something new. After all, it's easier to live with failure than to live with regret. You can e-mail me through my Web site at www.stephaniebond.com to let me know what happens. I'd love to hear from you.

Meanwhile, thank you for reading my books, and be sure to let friends know about the great love stories found between the pages of Harlequin romance novels!

Much love and laughter,

Stephanie Bond

STEPHANIE BOND

Just Dare Me...

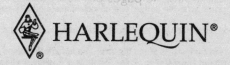

HARLEQUIN®

TORONTO • NEW YORK • LONDON
AMSTERDAM • PARIS • SYDNEY • HAMBURG
STOCKHOLM • ATHENS • TOKYO • MILAN • MADRID
PRAGUE • WARSAW • BUDAPEST • AUCKLAND

ISBN-13: 978-0-373-79286-3
ISBN-10: 0-373-79286-7

JUST DARE ME...

This edition published by arrangement with Harlequin Books S.A.

® and TM are trademarks of the publisher. Trademarks indicated with ® are registered in the United States Patent and Trademark Office, the Canadian Trade Marks Office and in other countries.

www.eHarlequin.com

Printed in U.S.A.

ABOUT THE AUTHOR

Stephanie Bond believes it's a privilege to write romance novels for the greatest, most loyal readers in the world. She lives with her architect/artist husband in her own happily-ever-after in Atlanta, Georgia, where chances are good that at this moment she is either reading a romance novel or writing one.

Books by Stephanie Bond

HARLEQUIN BLAZE
2—TWO SEXY!
169—MY FAVORITE MISTAKE

HARLEQUIN TEMPTATION
685—MANHUNTING IN MISSISSIPPI
718—CLUB CUPID
751—ABOUT LAST NIGHT…
769—IT TAKES A REBEL
787—TOO HOT TO SLEEP
805—SEEKING SINGLE MALE
964—COVER ME

MIRA BOOKS
BODY MOVERS

Many thanks to my editor, Brenda Chin,
for taking me on more than
one fun outdoor adventure!

And thanks to rugged outdoorsmen and
friends Steve Grantham and Phillip Giese
for giving me tips on various equipment.

Also, thanks to my dad for including me
in his paddling trips while I was growing up,
and for teaching me an appreciation and
respect for the outdoors.

Finally, this story is set in the gorgeous
Amicalola Falls area in the north Georgia
mountains. And although I've taken liberties
with the trail names and topography, I highly
recommend the area for hikers of all levels.

1

"So who do you think she slept with to get that promotion?"

Gabrielle Flannery tore her gaze away from the striking blonde in the front of the room, for whom the entire department had gathered for a send-off on a Friday afternoon, and frowned at her coworker, Tori. "Courtney has always been nice to me—and to you."

Tori snorted. "Yeah, because we catered to her like the servants we are."

Gabrielle shook her head at her friend and strained for a better view of the cake-cutting from where they stood behind a ficus tree in the crowded conference room. "Well, I, for one, am happy that Courtney is moving on to better things," she said, keeping her voice lowered.

"Yeah," Tori muttered. "A six-figure salary, a gargantuan expense account, a new company car and a corner office. Score another one for the cool kids, while we dweebs are still batting zero."

Gabrielle shifted uncomfortably at being included in the dweeb reference. "You're being unkind, Tori. We each contribute to the bottom line of this firm, we each have our own accounts." Her pulse picked up a notch as devilishly handsome Dell Kingston stepped up to say a few parting words about Courtney.

"Right," Tori said behind her hand. "Don't you think it's strange that all the high-profile, exciting products like sex-enhancement drugs and European cars go to people like Courtney Rodgers and Dell Kingston, and people like us get stuck with toilet paper and dog food?"

Gabrielle craned for a better view, although admittedly, the rugged profile of Dell Kingston was of more interest than the decorated sheet cake. "They have seniority," she murmured absently.

Tori scoffed. "Both of them came in two lousy weeks before we did, Gabrielle, and their careers are light years ahead of ours. Look at us," she said, swatting at a branch. "They're in the spotlight, and we're standing in a tree, spectators to their success."

Gabrielle bit into her lip, watching Courtney and Dell, the Barbie and Ken of Noble Marketing of Atlanta, smiling at each other as if they shared an intimate secret.

"Now that Courtney is leaving, Dell's going to be a free man," Tori whispered in Gabrielle's ear in a singsongy voice.

"Stop it." But a flush heated Gabrielle's neck and face—she wished she'd never shared her huge crush on Dell with Tori, and was glad she hadn't shared the true extent of her feelings for him. As if Dell Kingston would ever be interested in her, except as the butt of a joke. The man teased her mercilessly about her red hair and freckles, often assuming an outrageous Irish accent for good measure.

"May I have your attention, please?" Dell asked, bestowing his trademark grin on the group assembled.

The room grew quiet, and Gabrielle could feel every cell in her body straining toward him. The man was absolutely magnetic, with big, brown eyes that tied her tongue in knots.

He turned toward the beautiful Courtney. "We're gathered here today in the presence of these witnesses," he began, then stopped. "No, wait—that's only in my dreams."

Everyone groaned, then laughed as Courtney punched him lightly in the arm.

Gabrielle joined in the laughter halfheartedly, but inside, she succumbed to a pang of envy toward Courtney Rodgers—a tall, golden-haired, voluptuous beauty queen with a distinguished Southern pedigree. She'd used all of those assets to achieve her status as a top-notch manager of some of the firm's most prestigious accounts and parlayed them into a promotion to the New York office.

Although it was hard to fault the woman. Courtney put in long hours at Noble.

Then Gabrielle sighed inwardly—but not as many hours as she and Tori had put in.

"Seriously," Dell continued, comfortable at the center of attention, "we're all going to miss Courtney and we wish her only the best in her new adventure. Oh, and just so everyone knows—I have dibs on the CEG account."

Everyone laughed at Dell's good-natured arrogance.

"That account should be *yours,*" Tori whispered.

The CEG account—Cutting Edge Gear, a hot outdoor equipment account with an even hotter celebrity spokesman. The highlight of Gabrielle's career had been acting as Courtney's unofficial assistant on the account, hoping that someday she'd get to meet Nick Ocean, the movie-star spokesman. With Courtney leaving, Gabrielle had secretly entertained fantasies of their boss, Bruce Noble, offering her the account...but, of course, Dell would get it.

Dell said a few final words about Courtney and everyone applauded.

Courtney, who wasn't just leaving for a new job, but embarking on a new *adventure,* Gabrielle mused. For some people, every move they made seemed more exciting, more exotic than that of the average person.

The average *dweeb.*

Dell gave Courtney a hug, leaving his arm slung around her shoulders. Gabrielle leaned forward, wondering how people reached that magical place where the world seemed to fall at their feet. She wished she was fearless, exuded charm, had the nerve to go after what she wanted. How lucky the woman was to orbit in Dell's galaxy…to have him touching her…

Suddenly the potted tree in front of Gabrielle moved. No, she realized with horrific clarity—she was falling! Hugging the tree, she and the ficus both pitched forward and landed hard on the floor, soil spilling up her long skirt. Gasps sounded all around her, then laughter traveled around the room. Gabrielle rolled onto her back and closed her eyes, praying that everyone would ignore her—as usual—and that the festivities would continue.

"Gabrielle, for heaven's sake, your skirt is up to your shoulders," Tori hissed. "Mr. Noble is staring at you. Get up!"

The laughter gained momentum, although it sounded as if people were *trying* to muffle it with their hands. She lay there, eyes closed, limbs unresponsive, willing a blood clot to take her.

"Are you trying to upstage me?" a low voice murmured.

Gabrielle's eyes opened to see Dell Kingston

leaning over her, his rich, chocolate-brown eyes full of mirth.

"No," she croaked.

"Are you hurt?"

"No."

He reached down and pulled her to her feet. "Nothing to see here, folks," he said in a fake authoritative voice. "Move it along to the cake table, please."

Gabrielle's face flamed in humiliation as people filed past them. Mr. Noble squinted at her as if trying to recall her name. She brushed soil from her tan-colored tweed jacket. Her long matching skirt had fared worse, bearing dark, wet smears. Contrasted with the bright blue silk suit that Courtney wore, her own scratchy suit seemed worse than frumpy, and completely inappropriate for the summer heat.

"You sure you're okay?" Dell said, a smile curling his gorgeous mouth.

She nodded, mortified to have created such a spectacle. "I'm sorry."

"Don't be," he said with a laugh, then leaned in and murmured, "That's a nice pair of legs you've been hiding, Gabby."

Her mouth tightened—she hated that nickname. But a little thrill bolted through her at his compliment.

"Dell," Courtney called, "I need some help over here."

"Coming," he said, then he reached forward and touched his finger to the tip of Gabrielle's nose, coming away with a smudge of dirt. "Watch out for those attack trees."

Her throat convulsed at his close proximity. His features were strong and masculine, his short, dark hair sexily rumpled. His teeth were white against his bronze skin. His spicy cologne teased her nose. She couldn't have spoken if she tried.

So instead, she turned and fled for the exit.

DELL KINGSTON quirked a smile as he watched the slender redhead escape from the room—the woman was certainly good at disappearing. And she was a bit of a klutz, he thought wryly, remembering the times he'd rescued her from an overflowing coffee-pot, a copier machine that had gone on the offense and an avalanche of binders in the supply room. He righted the unfortunate tree, leaving mounds of dirt on the carpet.

He enjoyed teasing Gabby Flannery because she was so quick to blush, and didn't lash back like most of the women in the department. It was obvious that she was crushing on him, and he smiled at the thought of little Gabby lying awake at night fantasizing about him.

It was sweet, really.

Although there was nothing sweet about the

expanse of killer legs her tumble had exposed, or his gut-clenching reaction. He wondered idly what other secrets the flame-haired wallflower was hiding beneath those Puritan suits she wore, and just how daring the woman might be…in the right hands.

"Dell," Courtney sang, her voice lilting higher.

"Coming," he repeated, forcing his mind back to the happy occasion of Courtney's departure.

They'd passed some good times between the sheets, but otherwise he and the buxom blonde were woefully incompatible. Her leaving was a win-win situation—she was moving up to the company's Manhattan office, and he would have the coveted CEG account. With Courtney gone, no one else stood in his way. Gabby certainly didn't present a threat—with the encouragement of a well-placed wink or two, she'd pass along everything she'd learned about CEG from working on the fringes of the account…and perhaps would fall into the role of *his* unofficial assistant.

Then his mind flashed back to the image of Gabby Flannery lying on the floor, her long, lean legs parted, and he pushed his tongue into his cheek. With Courtney gone, he'd also need to find a new…pastime.

And suddenly the idea of a blushing, tongue-tied, *useful* redhead in his bed was tremendously appealing.

2

GABRIELLE JOGGED to her cubicle, furious with herself for creating a scene that would make her the laughingstock of the office, yet again.

Tori was right—she *was* a dweeb.

"Hey, Gabrielle," her friend called behind her. "Wait up!"

But Gabrielle marched into her cube, and grabbed her briefcase and purse. If she left now, she wouldn't have to stand on the elevator with her coworkers.

"It wasn't that bad," Tori said, then she lost the battle and a burst of laughter filtered through her fingers. "Okay, that was hilarious, stealing Courtney's thunder."

Gabrielle expelled a frustrated sigh. "Tori, I didn't do it on purpose!"

"That's not the way I'm going to tell it," Tori said with a grin.

Gabrielle swung her purse strap to her shoulder. "I'm going home."

"But it's Friday," Tori pouted. "We're supposed to volunteer usher at the Fox Theater."

Them and every senior citizen in midtown—God, *this* was her social life. "Not tonight. I'll call you sometime this weekend."

Tori clasped her arm. "Are you okay? I mean, it's not like you haven't made a fool out of yourself before—" Then she stopped, her eyes wide. "I didn't mean that the way it sounded."

Gabrielle blinked back moisture and looked down at her stained, outdated suit, replaying the mortifying incident in the conference room and, worse, her stuttering and sputtering around Dell, who always made her feel inept and unattractive. A few months from turning thirty, and in the face of pressure, she regressed to the gawky teenager who had been the punch line of every joke in high school. Lying on the floor with potting soil up her skirt and all her coworkers laughing, she had seen her career pass before her eyes. She would never be in the league of Dell Kingston or Courtney Rodgers. Once a dweeb, always a dweeb.

"Have fun at the Fox, Tori."

She headed toward the elevator, her shoulders hunched, her hands in her pockets.

"Gabrielle!" Tori called behind her. "Don't be like that!"

She stared straight ahead as she rode down in the

elevator, then walked outside into the summer heat shimmering off the sidewalks in downtown Atlanta. But her friend's words looped in her head as she waited at the Marta stop for the bus that would take her to the station a few blocks from her cramped midtown apartment. *Don't be like that...don't dream big...don't be offended when people over-look you...underestimate you...ignore you.*

In the muggy July temperatures, she was mis-erable in her dirty, wooly suit. When the bus lurched to a halt, she climbed on with other work-weary passengers. Predictably, within a few minutes, the bus was trapped in Friday gridlock traffic.

The traffic, she thought wryly, was symbolic of her career—at a complete standstill.

She loved the field of work she'd chosen, and believed that Noble was one of the industry's best firms, but she'd had higher hopes for her career. Noble had always been a firm she could see herself retiring from...but she had horrible visions of herself thirty years from now, still a junior account exec, still standing behind the plants at staff gatherings.

As the relatively short drive extended longer and longer, she looked for something to take her mind off the troublesome thoughts about herself. On the seat next to her lay a copy of *U.S. Weekly Review.* She picked it up and leafed through the bent pages, stopping on an article titled Adrenaline Rush—

Change Your Mind, Change Your Life. Intrigued, she started reading the article that asserted most people encountered some sort of plateau in their life, and the only way to get things moving was to harness the mind's energy and take a risk.

In your mind's eye, picture what it is that you want, then ask yourself, if you go for it, what's the worst thing that could happen? You can recover from anything short of death, and if you fail, you probably won't be worse off. But if you rally your talents and your inner strength, chances are you won't fail; in fact, you are likely to succeed beyond your wildest dreams.

Gabrielle sat up straighter in her seat, her chest suffused with the strange, prickly feeling that the magazine article was written especially for her. *Change your mind, change your life, take a risk.*

When was the last time she'd experienced an adrenaline rush? In the evenings, she either worked late or brought work home, which had ceased to be exciting years ago. On weekends she did her volunteer stint at the Fox Theater, which required wearing a red-and-black outfit and showing people to their seats in exchange for sitting in an empty seat or on the stairs to watch the shows for free. She hadn't dated since...a long time ago. The only special people in her life were Tori, who could be a bit of a downer, and McGee, who wasn't even a person, but her pet bulldog.

She sighed, conceding that the only adrenal activity she'd experienced lately was when she passed Dell Kingston in the hallway, or the times he had saved her from some bumbling mess she'd gotten herself into.

God, how pathetic that the most exciting thing in her life was a reaction to someone else—someone who barely acknowledged her existence. Other women her age, like Courtney, were creating excitement in their lives by proactively stepping out of their comfort zone and trying something new.

It was time she took control of her life, she decided, lifting her chin.

Then she bit into her lip—but how?

She scanned the article again. *In your mind's eye, picture what it is that you want, then ask yourself, if you go for it, what's the worst thing that could happen?*

What did she want? she asked herself. What would make her happy? To be noticed…to be recognized…to be given the opportunity to showcase her brains and her talents…

She wanted the CEG account.

The bus stopped and the doors opened at the midtown station. Gabrielle stuffed the magazine in her bag and disembarked, her mind clicking. "I want the CEG account," she said aloud, testing the words on her tongue.

But you heard Dell…he has designs on the CEG account…of course Bruce Noble will give it to him, her subconscious whispered. It was crazy to think that the boss would hand over one of the firm's most lucrative accounts to her, especially after witnessing her spectacle today.

On the other hand, with Courtney leaving, she was the person who was most acquainted with CEG and its products—she had worked with the product engineers to understand the specs of each piece of outdoor equipment and helped to create brochures to highlight the premium features that CEG wanted to stress to consumers.

She climbed the stairs to her fourth-floor one-bedroom apartment. Hadn't she walked up and down these very stairs for hours to test CEG hiking boots so she could better understand how they functioned?

She unlocked the door to her apartment, smiling and crouching down to hug McGee and rub his little, flat face. After promising him a walk as soon as she changed, she glanced around her crowded apartment with a frown.

And hadn't she dedicated much of her and McGee's living space to CEG products—tents, backpacks, rappelling equipment and camping gear?

With McGee at her heels, she raised her hands and grabbed onto a metal T-bar, then lifted her feet to ride a cabled zip line down the hall—another CEG product—to her bedroom. She put her feet down and set her purse and briefcase on the end of the cluttered bed, unused for the past three months because she'd been testing the comfort of a CEG tent pitched in the living room.

A sigh escaped her as she glanced at the clothes piled on the bed. And hadn't she given up most of her closet space to CEG workout clothes and running gear?

She didn't spend the weekends defying death, like Dell Kingston was purported to have done with his rock climbing and acrobatic rappelling and triathlons. But she'd analyzed the products, studied the specs and knew the limitations. She'd bet that she knew at least as much about CEG products as Dell did.

"I want the CEG account," she repeated, this time with more force.

McGee barked his enthusiastic agreement.

She slowly undressed, peeling her sticky blouse from her body, and bypassed her dry cleaner's bag in favor of the trash can for her soiled, dated suit. She pulled on shorts and a T-shirt, using her hand to smooth down the loose bits of hair that stuck up from her French braid. Good grief, the stuff was like an unruly scouring pad.

If you go for it, what's the worst thing that could happen?

She'd be humiliated and have to slink back to her cubicle and be satisfied with her feminine hygiene and hemorrhoid cream accounts. Although, would it really be any more humiliating to be turned down by Bruce Noble than wrestling with a tree in front of the entire department—and losing?

No, she decided. But would she be able to talk to Bruce Noble without lapsing into a babbling fool? She glanced at the discarded suit, which McGee was sniffing suspiciously. And if she were going to step into Courtney's shoes, she had to step up her wardrobe a notch. Or three.

Gabrielle reached into the back of her closet and removed a pale green suit that her mother had given her for her birthday. Fiona Flannery was a flamboyant redhead who was always pushing her daughter to play up her unusual coloring, frequently sending makeup and beauty products and clothes that Gabrielle hadn't had the nerve to use or wear.

She held the suit in front of her and stared at her reflection in the closet door mirror. The fabric was soft and clingy, the color set off her green eyes. The jacket was fitted and flirty, the skirt was short—well above the knee.

Remembering Dell's comment about her long, albino legs, her cheeks warmed. He'd only been teasing her, of course, trying to get a rise out of her. But it was fun to think that maybe the flash in his decadent eyes had been a tiny bit of male appreciation.

Then she smirked at her reflection. If Dell got wind of her vying for the CEG account, would he feel threatened...or would he laugh?

What's the worst that can happen?

She could always go back to being invisible.

She put a leash on McGee and pulled the magazine out of her bag to take on their walk. McGee was the dearest dog ever created, but he moved his squatty little self like a sleepy snail—a turn around the block gave her plenty of time to reread the "Adrenaline Rush" article for tips on how to begin working toward her goal.

To prepare for an uncomfortable situation, visualize the scene, how you want it to unfold, how you will respond to resistance. Write a script, and practice what you'll say until you can speak with authority.

Visualize...practice...

She closed her eyes and with great effort, banished the vision of her walking into Bruce Noble's office Monday morning, her knees quaking, her voice leaving her. Instead, she visualized walking into his office Monday morning, declining his offer to sit, calling him "Bruce," and telling him that she wanted—no, that she *deserved*—the CEG account.

But each time she visualized Bruce's face, he looked incredulous, skeptical and stupefied at her request.

But when she returned to her apartment, now carrying McGee because he couldn't maneuver the stairs, an idea popped into her head. She rifled through her briefcase, and pulled out the company's full-color annual report. Inside was a picture of Bruce Noble, his face nearly life-size...and smiling. She tore out the photo and pasted it onto a piece of cardboard, then cut along the outline of his face. Then she fastened the cardboard face to the front of a ball cap.

"McGee, come here, sweetie."

He lumbered over and stood patiently while she settled the cap onto his meaty head.

"Perfect," she said, then stepped back to stare at Bruce Noble's smiling face. "Mr. Noble, I want the CEG account."

McGee barked, his jowls bouncing, not unlike her boss's.

"Why?" She picked up the green suit and held it against her. "Because I've assisted on the account for two years—I know the products, I wrote most of the literature, and..."

McGee barked, as if prompting her.

She pulled the clasp from her braid and ran her fingers through her long hair, releasing it into all its furious glory. "*And* I deserve this chance…Bruce. I've given this firm six years of my life, and I'm good at my job. Just as good at Dell Kingston. And I'm tired of being overlooked…by everyone."

The memory of Dell's mocking smile as he'd pulled her to her feet flooded her with stinging humiliation all over again. He'd teased her, dismissed her, just like the others.

But Monday morning, she thought determinedly, she would be noticed…for all the *right* reasons.

3

DELL PRESSED the elevator button and drank deeply from his large cup of coffee, trying to wake up. He'd gone mountain biking yesterday morning in the summer heat, then spent the afternoon rock climbing. It had seemed worthwhile—even enjoyable—at the time, but this morning his ass was dragging and his joints moaning.

He nodded to the security guard, the only other person in the lobby at this early hour. But Bruce Noble was always in his office before most people were out of bed, and Dell had decided to use the opportunity to formally request the CEG account. Formally because it was a near certainty that he would get it—he was a senior account executive with an impeccable track record. And CEG was a perfect fit for him because he spent most of his free time outdoors pushing his body to new limits.

Plus, stuffing his resume with A-list accounts was the shortest route to success.

Success meant early retirement.

Early retirement meant having the time to do the things he enjoyed most.

Ergo, CEG was an important brick in his career path.

Still, he didn't want to appear presumptuous. It was best to follow protocol and plead his case to Noble so that there would be no misunderstandings.

The elevator doors opened and he stepped inside. Behind him he heard the click of high heels on the tile floor, a sound that always spiked his pulse.

"Hold the elevator," a female voice called.

He pressed the open button, then looked up to see a tall, leggy woman stride across the lobby like a beautiful colt, her slender figure clad in a trendy green suit, her long legs extended farther by a pair of those high-heeled, pointy-toed shoes that made his cock jump. God, he loved those on women.

She walked into the car and murmured, "Thank you."

He took a deep drink from his cup to cover his frank perusal of the beauty next to him. Her hair was the color of a red maple tree in full fall flame—spectacular.

Damn, what was it about redheads lately that had him so worked up?

Actually, except for the fact that this woman was polished to a professional shine, her makeup glamorous, her posture self-assured, she reminded him a little of...

He inhaled a mouthful of scalding coffee and sputtered like a car engine. "Gabby?" he gasped.

She turned to him, eyebrows arched over the most gorgeous green eyes he'd ever seen. "Yes?"

He blinked. Wait a minute—he *had* seen those eyes before, only...were her lashes always so long, her mouth always so wide and inviting? "You look...wow," he said, stumbling over his words.

The blush that pinked her cheeks was the first sign of the old Gabby. "Were you planning to push the button for our floor?"

Feeling like an idiot, he stabbed at it three times before it lit up.

"Did you have a nice weekend?" he asked, still reeling.

"Yes, thank you," she responded, tucking a long lock of hair behind a delicate ear.

As they climbed, he tried not to stare, but couldn't drag his gaze away from her profile. The transformation from ugly duckling to siren swan was just short of miraculous.

Desire swelled in his midsection and suddenly, the prospect of Gabby assisting him on the CEG account held even more promise. And she must be entertaining similar thoughts of a *collaboration,* he reasoned with smug satisfaction, or else why would she be dressed like that?

The elevator doors opened and she walked out in front of him.

"Um, Gabby," he said.

She turned back. "Yes?"

"I've been meaning to talk to you about the CEG account."

"What about it?"

He pulled out his most charming smile. "Well, I'm going to need some…help. And I know that Courtney found you indispensable."

The tightening of her mouth told him that Courtney had not been that forthcoming with her about her value.

"I was hoping you'd be willing to share your expertise with me, now that I'll be taking over the account."

Her eyes clouded slightly. "Has Mr. Noble officially assigned the CEG account to you?"

"No…not officially," he felt obligated to say. "Actually, that's why I came in early, to talk to him about it."

A small smile curved her mouth. "What a coincidence." Then she turned and walked away from him.

Dell stood there nodding, too distracted by the swing of her shapely backside to fully comprehend her words. Then he blinked—what had she said? Something about a coincidence?

His eyes widened. Surely she didn't mean... He scoffed—she couldn't possibly think...

Alarm blipped through his chest when he realized that Gabby hadn't gone in the direction of her cubicle, but in the direction of Bruce Noble's office!

GABRIELLE STOPPED at the closed door of Bruce's office, inhaled deeply and knocked. She was feeling more than a little off-kilter from her encounter with Dell, but she had to focus on her goal.

"Come in," Bruce called.

She drew on the strength of a weekend of rehearsing with an amiable Bruce Noble cutout that followed her around the apartment and smiled at her across the kitchen table, while she picked at her microwave entrees and McGee munched the kibble in his doggie dish. She could do this. With a deep inhale, she opened the door and walked in.

"Good morning, Bruce."

Her boss squinted at her, then his eyes flew open. "Ms. Flannery?"

"I hope I'm not disturbing you."

"Er, no...what can I do for you?"

She looked at his smiling face and as she'd practiced a thousand times said, "Bruce, I want the CEG account."

She braced for his reaction—confusion, derision, belly laughter. Instead, Bruce removed his glasses and set them aside. "The CEG account. Well, I have to admit, Gabrielle, this is a surprise…but a welcome one."

A short rap on the door sounded, followed by Dell Kingston walking in. "Good morning, Bruce."

Gabrielle set her jaw at the intrusion.

"Morning, Dell. Ms. Flannery and I were just talking about the CEG account."

She caught the flash of panic in Dell's eyes before it was replaced by cool confidence. "Oh, good. Because I was thinking that Gabby should be given the official title of assistant on the account."

Bruce pursed his mouth. "You do?"

"Absolutely," Dell said magnanimously.

"Gabrielle thinks that she should be given full responsibility of CEG."

Dell emitted a good-natured laugh that stiffened her spine. "No offense, but I don't think that Gabby's ready to take on a client as high-maintenance as CEG."

"You mean as important?" Gabrielle said, crossing her arms.

Dell conceded with a nod, splaying his hands wide.

Under Dell's penetrating gaze, a hot flush began climbing her neck. For a few seconds, her mind whirled in desperation as the familiar speechlessness threatened to overtake her. With great effort, she dragged her gaze away from Dell's and back to the smiling face that had watched television with her and chased a tennis ball around the apartment.

"I've devoted six years to this firm," she said, her voice steady. "I've worked with some of the most obscure, unusual and difficult products in our lineup, and the clients have always been pleased."

Bruce nodded in agreement, and it was all she could do not to pet his head.

"I want this account," she added, lifting her chin. "I know the products inside and out. I designed the advertising literature and wrote most of the copy. I suggested and managed the overhaul of the online store."

Dell scoffed. "Desk work is one thing, Bruce, but you know the people at CEG—they're outdoorsmen, and so am I. When I'm not here, I'm mountain biking, hiking, climbing, rappelling, you name it. I *live* this stuff."

Bruce looked to Gabrielle, seemingly waiting for more ammunition.

She swallowed hard. "I've worn out the stairs in my apartment building, personally testing CEG backpacks and hiking boots. And for the past three months I've slept in one of their tents pitched in the living room of my apartment."

Both sets of male eyebrows shot up at her pronouncement, then Bruce's phone rang. He glanced at the console. "Excuse me for a minute, I need to take this call."

Gabrielle turned and reached for the door, but Dell beat her there and held it open for her. She glared at him, then walked through. Out in the hall, the tension between them was palpable. She tried to tamp down her nervousness, telling herself that she had presented her case well. Bruce hadn't laughed at her, hadn't dismissed her, hadn't reminded her that last week he and everyone else had seen her tighty-whitey underwear.

Then Dell's soft laugh caught her attention. He looked conciliatory. "Gabby, come on, you don't really expect Bruce to give you CEG. Why don't you just stick to the feminine hygiene products and leave CEG to someone who can handle it?"

In that instant, her heart shriveled. She realized that all the times Dell had been flirtatiously teasing her, inside he'd been laughing at her clumsiness and labeling her as incompetent. He truly didn't think she was capable of competing on his level. If he knew how she'd fallen for him over those fleeting shared moments, he'd have an even bigger laugh at her expense.

She felt like a fool. Her wounded pride threatened to disable her, but she hardened her jaw and spoke through clenched teeth. "My name is *Gabrielle*. And no matter what Bruce decides, please don't patronize me, Dell."

Something unrecognizable flared in his eyes—hostility? Resentment?

Bruce's door suddenly swung open and he beckoned them both inside. Gabrielle preceded Dell, her body stiff, and wondered if she'd be able to back up the statements rolling out of her mouth, which seemed to have a mind of its own this morning.

That darn magazine article had blown her up with false bravado. If Bruce gave the account to Dell and asked her to assist, she'd be stuck working with Dell under rather *tense* circumstances.

Bruce Noble leaned against the front of his desk, his arms folded. "I just got off the phone with Eddie Fosser at CEG. He also wants to know who'll be taking over the account. I told him my dilemma." He gestured toward Dell. "On one hand I have a senior account executive who would fit nicely into the CEG corporate environment."

Dell smiled, and Gabrielle seethed. "Fit in," meaning a testosterone-laden male.

Then Bruce gestured to her. "On the other hand I have a junior account executive who is familiar with the client's products and might have been, er—" he coughed "—inadvertently overlooked for past opportunities."

Gabrielle smiled—maybe Bruce was going to do the right thing after all.

"So Eddie and I were talking, and he suggested

something that might give you both a chance to prove yourselves."

She and Dell exchanged a puzzled glance, and she felt some measure of relief that apparently he didn't know what their boss had in mind.

"CEG is sponsoring a wilderness survival trip this weekend in the Georgia mountains with their celebrity spokesman. Eddie will be there with some other CEG execs, and a couple of their big customers. It's a good-natured competition to showcase their products, with each player accumulating points. Eddie suggested that both of you attend and…whichever one of you scores the highest will get the account."

A vacuum of silence pulled at her ears.

"This is based on athletic ability?" Dell asked, shooting an amused smile in her direction.

"Well, certainly athleticism will help," Bruce said, "but it's more like a test of wills…and logic. And it'll give you a chance to interact with Eddie and his people." Bruce clapped his hands together. "I think it's a great idea. It's on the Amicalola Falls State Park property. You'd leave Thursday and return Monday. What do you say?"

Gabrielle felt like an animal trapped in a searchlight…in a tree…having sex…upside down. Compete with Dell in a wilderness survival weekend? There must be thousands of ways for him to humiliate her in the woods.

"I think it's a great idea, too," Dell said, then turned to Gabrielle, his eyes alight with predetermined victory, his mouth barely able to contain a grin. "But if you're not up to it, *Gabrielle,* then just say so and we'll go back to the original arrangement—I'll take the lead on the account, and you'll be my assistant."

She swallowed hard, her mind racing over the advice in the "Adrenaline Rush" article.

Then Dell lowered his head and leaned slightly toward her. "Come on, Gabby," he whispered in a taunting voice for her ears only. "I dare you."

At his challenging words, an unfamiliar strength swelled in her chest—at least she hoped it was strength, and not a reaction to the fact that for the first time, Dell would have to deal with her as a rival, a competitor, a peer.

The article had described moments like this—when a person's life choices, past and future, seemed to converge into one decision that had to be made on gut instinct and self-trust.

She looked Dell Kingston square in his dreamy eyes and, after almost faltering under the sheer impact of his sexy gaze, she found her voice. "You're on."

A cocky grin split his face and he extended his hand to her. "Then may the best man—or woman—win."

She stared at his large hand before clasping it with her own, unprepared for the shock of his warm fingers swallowing hers. His gaze raked her up and down, taking in every inch of the exterior she'd carefully constructed over the weekend—a facade of confidence that shook precariously when Dell looked at her that way…the way a man looked at a woman.

On a challenge bolstered by a silly dare, she'd agreed to spend four days in the woods with this man.

And four nights.

And something in his never-ending eyes told her that with all the dangers in the wild, Dell Kingston himself posed the biggest threat to her well-being…and to her state of mind.

4

"I STILL THINK you've lost your freaking mind," Tori said, her eyes bleary, her sleep-mussed hair sticking up at all angles. "First you go through some Stepford executive makeover, and now you're heading off to the mountains with…that man."

"We've been over this," Gabrielle said, handing over McGee, who squirmed in Tori's unfamiliar arms. "I have to do this to get the CEG account."

"I don't know why that stupid account is so important to you."

Detecting a note of abandonment in her friend's voice, she laid a hand on her arm. "Tori, you were the one who pointed out the inequity of the account assignments. I'm only fighting for what I deserve."

But instead of cheering up, Tori only looked more morose. "I've seen documentaries on these wilderness survival trips—they lure you in with romantic notions of sitting around the campfire, and the next thing you know, you're running for your life, being hunted by some guy with a crossbow."

Gabrielle squinted. "You watch way too much television. And I assure you, there were no romantic promises. I'm expecting the worst—eating bugs, dangling from cliffs—"

"Sharing a tent with Dell Kingston."

Gabrielle blinked. "*What?* Now who's lost their mind?"

"That's what everyone in the office is saying," Tori said, her voice tinged with a gossipy tone. "That Dell is going to get the CEG account *and* get into your pants."

Anger flared in her chest. "Well, they're wrong, and you can tell them so."

"Just be careful," Tori said earnestly. "I know how you feel about Dell—"

"I don't—"

"I *know* how you feel about Dell, and I just don't want you to do something that you'll regret."

Gabrielle inhaled a calming breath, trying not to let her friend's comments make her any more nervous about the long drive into the mountains with Dell that stretched ahead of her. She'd never missed having a car before today. She closed her eyes against the image of his dancing brown eyes. *Come on, Gabby. I dare you.*

"Trust me," she said forcefully, for her benefit and for Tori's, "Dell Kingston has nothing on his mind for this weekend except scoring higher than me on the competition."

"I'd say you're right about one thing," Tori said dryly. "His mind is on scoring, all right."

Gabrielle massaged her temples—this she did not need. "Are you sure you don't mind taking care of McGee?"

"We'll be fine until you get back. Hey, have you ever noticed that McGee looks a little like Mr. Noble?"

"You think?" Gabrielle said, backing down the stairs and shoving on her sunglasses. "I'll call you if my cell phone works in the mountains."

"Good luck," Tori yelled. "Get Nick Ocean's autograph for me. And keep your tent flap closed!"

DELL CHECKED his watch, then glanced at the front of the Marta station for the hundredth time. Had he missed her? Considering the color of her hair, he didn't think that was possible.

And considering her flair for misadventure, she might be lying at the bottom of a set of stairs somewhere, or hanging from a flag pole. The pale slip of a woman would be lucky to make it through the weekend without breaking her lovely neck. Still, he shook his head, smiling at Bruce's genius. The man couldn't flat-out deny Gabby's request for the account without Human Resources climbing all over him. A competition was the perfect way to give Dell the account without making it look so obvious.

And Gabby had nearly conceded on the spot—he'd seen it in her eyes. He still wasn't sure what had driven him to dare her to accept the challenge. Something about the woman had always piqued his interest, even before her transformation. Gabby had this air of aloof independence that made him want to rankle her. Her pluckiness intrigued him. He could have walked out of Bruce's office with CEG in his pocket. But this way, he told himself, she'd feel as if she'd given it her best shot, and would be more willing to assist on the account. And it would give her a chance to warm up to him.

There was only one problem—

A flash of red caught his attention and sure enough, it was Gabby, dressed in loose cargo pants and a white T-shirt, her blazing hair pulled back into a long, thick ponytail. She struggled to stand upright with the large backpack strapped to her slender body. God, she looked so young and vulnerable and…sexy.

The problem that had been gnawing at him all week hit him full force, causing him to shift in his seat. Little Gabby Flannery had always been a curiosity to him, but over the past few days in the office, every glimpse of her in her new slim suits and short skirts, with her hair flowing wild around her shoulders, had him setting his jaw against an unexpected surge of lust.

How he was going to keep his hands to himself during four days of close contact with her in the great outdoors while trying to make sure she didn't kill herself, he didn't know.

He climbed out of his SUV and waved. She smiled and lifted her hand, but the movement threw her off balance and sent her stumbling backward to sit down hard on the sidewalk.

He rolled his eyes and hurried across the street to help her. "Are you okay?"

She looked up and nodded, fumbling with the straps of the backpack across her chest.

"Let me," he said, then unfastened the straps, willing himself to ignore the incidental contact with her full breasts.

This was not a promising start.

When she was free, he helped her to her feet and picked up her pack, wincing at its weight. "Christ, do you have a body in here?"

"No," she murmured. "Just trying to cover all the bases."

"Let me guess—high heels and makeup?"

She frowned. "No."

He winked, then headed toward his SUV. "You're late, we need to get on the road."

"Sorry. I had to drop my dog off at Tori's, and the trains were delayed."

"Do you have one of those Tinkerbell dogs?"

She gave a little laugh that he liked the sound of. "McGee is a bulldog, and I don't think he'd take kindly to being called a Tinkerbell."

"Nice name," he said grudgingly, surprised that she would own such a substantial canine. He'd always wanted a dog himself, but his hectic travel schedule had always prevented him from owning one...at least that was his excuse, he acknowledged wryly.

He loaded her backpack into the rear of his vehicle, next to his own pack, which was half the size and weight. He'd been camping and hiking enough to know that most people packed too much gear. "So your friend, Tori...she's a little gloomy."

"She doesn't like you, either," Gabrielle said, climbing into the passenger seat and closing the door with a bang.

He frowned, then swung up into his own seat. "I didn't say I didn't like her."

"It's okay," Gabrielle said matter-of-factly. "We're used to it."

"Used to what?"

"Used to being ignored by the senior account execs."

He sputtered. "We don't ignore the junior account managers."

"Really? What's the name of the guy who sits in the cube next to mine?"

"The new guy?"

"He's worked there for five years."

"Oh…right." Dell tried to conjure up the man's face in his mind. "Mike something?"

"Close—Oscar. Oscar White. Nice guys with two kids, puts in about seventy hours a week at the office."

"Oh. Well, I guess our paths haven't crossed that much."

Her mouth flattened, and she remained infuriatingly quiet.

He started the engine and tried another tack as he pulled away from the curb. "So do you live around here?"

"No, I was coming from my friend's place. I live in Midtown."

"Really? So do I."

"I know. I've seen you at my grocery Sunday mornings."

"Why haven't you ever said hello?"

"You were always with a woman. Sometimes Courtney, sometimes…not."

He squirmed and inexplicably, he thought of Gabby waking up in his bed on Sunday morning and them running to the store for a newspaper and a carton of juice. The image very nearly made him miss the ramp to the interstate that would take them north toward the Georgia Mountains.

"I've seen you at the Fox Theater, too," she said.

"Oh? Do you moonlight at the Fox?"

"I'm a volunteer usher."

"Really? I thought only old people did that." He winced as soon as the words left his mouth.

"Old people and me," she said cheerfully.

How did she do that—keep him off balance, make him feel as if he were a snob? "I guess that's a great way to see all the shows."

She nodded and turned to look out the window. He hadn't given much thought to her salary, but he vaguely remembered being on a tight budget back when he'd been a junior account manager. There had been no money for theater tickets.

"How old are you, Gabby?"

After a few minutes of silence, she said, "I really wish you wouldn't call me that."

He gave a little laugh. "I think it's cute."

"I don't want to be cute," she said stiffly. "I want to be taken seriously. You think I don't know what everyone is saying?"

"What is everyone saying?"

"That this competition is a joke, that there's no way I can beat a superjock like you on a wilderness survival course."

He weighed his words, especially since he might have inadvertently fueled a few of those sentiments going round the office. "Apparently Bruce feels differently." His conscience plucked at him, though, for giving her false hope that she could actually beat him. After all, the woman had nearly been done in with her backpack.

She fell silent again, watching the passing scenery on Georgia 400 until they were north of the city. Dell couldn't remember a time when he'd actually *wanted* a woman to talk.

"Where are you from?" he asked finally.

"I grew up in a small town outside Chattanooga."

A small-town girl—not surprising. "Sounds nice. Are your parents still there?"

She nodded.

When no other information seemed forthcoming, he offered, "I grew up in D.C."

"I know. I helped to put together the bios for the senior account execs for the annual report. Your parents work for the Pentagon and you have an MBA from Emory."

What his bio didn't say was that his parents were bitterly disappointed that he hadn't gone into law or politics, that marketing had been a compromise of his skills and their expectations. Still, she knew more about him than he knew about her. Normally, that wouldn't bother him, but for some reason, he felt compelled to know what made this woman tick, why she was so spirited in spite of her social clumsiness.

After knocking over that tree in the conference room and sprawling in the floor, most people would have been too embarrassed to show their face again, much less have the balls to march into Bruce's office and ask for an A-list account.

"I think it's about a two-hour drive to Amicalola Falls," he said.

"More like three, actually." She pulled a sheaf of papers from one of the pockets in her cargo pants. "I'm a bit directionally impaired, but I read the information that Bruce gave us very carefully."

Of course she had. "Then maybe you can tell me what we're in for."

"The instructions aren't that specific, just that we should bring a stocked backpack, study the weather forecast and be prepared for anything."

Weather forecast. He looked toward the sky. Hmm, maybe he should have read those papers after all.

"A guide will meet us at the site and give us more instructions from there." She ran her finger down one of the sheets. "Says here there'll be ten of us."

He frowned. Not enough bodies to keep them from bumping into each other.

She pivoted her head. "Do you know Nick Ocean?"

Oh, brother—he knew that look. He'd seen it in Courtney's eyes when she talked about the movie star. "I've met him a couple of times at trade shows."

"What's he like? He seems so macho onscreen."

Dell shrugged and shifted in his seat. "I guess."

"Tori wants me to get his autograph."

"Just be careful around him. I've heard that he likes to hit on young women."

"That's funny," she murmured, looking back to the papers. "I've heard the same thing about you."

He frowned and only the ringing of his cell phone in its mounted cradle kept him from defending himself. In deference to the ban on holding a cell phone while driving, he hit the hands-free speaker button on the visor. "This is Dell."

"Hey, gorgeous, it's Courtney."

He glanced sideways at Gabby. She didn't act as if she were listening, but he wished he'd remembered to bring the headset for his phone. "Hi. This is a surprise."

"I just called to wish you luck on your wilderness weekend—wink, wink." She laughed gaily.

He shifted in his seat. "Uh, thanks. We're on our way up there now."

"We?"

"Gabby—I mean, Gabrielle is with me."

"Oh."

"She doesn't have a car."

"I see," she said, her voice laced with innuendo. "Well, Gabby, should feel right at home in the mountains, with all the *trees*." Laughter at her own joke burst over the speaker.

Dell shifted in his seat. "Courtney, you're on hands-free speaker."

"Oh. Sorry, Gabby," she said, not sounding sorry at all.

"How are things in Manhattan?" he asked, trying to reroute the conversation into safer territory.

"Great," she said brightly. "My apartment is fabulous, the view from my office is unreal and the men here think my southern accent is exotic."

"That's nice," he said breezily.

"In fact, I need to run. Have fun this weekend you two," she said, her voice singsongy. "Don't do anything I wouldn't do."

Thinking sourly that Courtney's parting remark left way too much leeway, Dell disconnected the call. "Sorry about that," he said, feeling annoyed with Courtney over her insensitive remarks, and feeling guilty that she had struck a nerve implying that in a cozy setting with a member of the opposite sex, he would behave accordingly.

Gabby didn't respond, just kept reading, which only disgruntled him more. Why wouldn't the woman talk to him? She just sat there, exuding some kind of light, fruity scent that made him wonder if she tasted as good as she smelled.

He wondered if she had any idea of how appealing she was, if she'd ever been thoroughly kissed or if she'd ever had those long, fabulous legs of hers wrapped around a man who knew what he was doing.

Then Dell pulled his hand down his face. He had

to get a grip on himself. These unforeseen feelings of lust were messing with his head.

He glanced at Gabby's tempting profile, groaning inwardly.

And they weren't even there yet.

5

GABRIELLE TRIED to concentrate on the papers she was pretending to read, wishing that she hadn't been privy to a conversation between Dell and his ex-whatever. And the last thing she needed was for Courtney to taunt her about the two of them being thrown together in an intimate setting. As if she weren't supremely aware of the man sitting next to her.

His seemingly constant questions had rattled her, but in truth, she preferred him talking—when she was answering him, it took her mind off the fact that he looked so sexy in his khaki shorts and pale blue T-shirt. Her gaze kept straying to his tanned, bare arms and legs, thinking how much more at ease he looked in hiking clothes versus suits.

Maybe *he* was more at ease, but seeing his muscular limbs sprawled in the seat and the athletic way he controlled his body was causing *her* a great deal of discomfort. And she couldn't afford to let her irrational attraction to Dell distract her from the competition—she needed all her faculties if she were going to have a fighting chance. With every mile that ticked off the odometer, the stone of dread in her stomach grew heavier and heavier. She nibbled on her thumbnail—what had she gotten herself into?

Dell seemed to have picked up speed since his phone call with Courtney. He turned off the state highway onto a two-lane road that led to the Amicalola Falls State Park, and with the change in landscape, her nerves ratcheted higher. Hoping to calm herself, she pulled out the "Adrenaline Rush" article that she'd torn out and brought with her for moral support.

> Everyone has untapped talents, or talents that you take for granted and can apply to other parts of your life.

She reread the words she'd already practically memorized, desperate to drum last-minute courage into her brain, but her brain seemed a little...woozy. Maybe it was her imagination, but the roads seemed to be getting more steep...and more curvy...

Suddenly her stomach roiled and she grabbed the handle on the door frame above her.

"What's wrong?" Dell asked.

"I...think...I'm...carsick," she murmured. "You might...want to...slow down."

"You might want to stop reading," he said irritably. "We're running late, remember?"

"I...don't...ride...in cars...very...often," she said, grabbing her stomach.

"Oh, good grief," he muttered.

The vehicle slowed, and he zoomed her window down, bathing her with hot, but fresh, air. She hung her head out the window and breathed deeply, knowing that she probably looked pathetic to Dell, but acknowledged it was better than throwing up in front of him. Several minutes later, her stomach was feeling a touch better...but her throat was feeling scratchy and her nose had started to run.

Ragweed.

Getting back to nature had brought her dormant allergies roaring to life. This did not bode well for the weekend. "Do you have a tissue?" she asked, wiping at her watery eyes.

He tapped the brake. "Are you going to be sick?"

"No, at least not yet. My allergies are acting up."

"Check the glove compartment," he said, pointing.

She opened it and a box of condoms sprang into her hand. There was also a black bra, a jock strap and a jar of something called Slippery Sex. The man drove a rolling love shack.

He grinned and didn't even have the grace to look sheepish. "In the back."

With her face burning, she rummaged past a

couple of maps, found a wad of napkins from a fast-food place, yanked one out and sneezed into it. She wanted to roll up the window, but didn't dare until the queasiness passed. "Please slow down," she moaned, resting her chin on the window opening.

"I'm going below the minimum speed limit," he said. "At this rate, we'll never get up this mountain." But he eased off the gas and waved two vehicles around them. When two bicyclists passed them going uphill, Dell's frustration became palpable.

"Maybe I should take you back," he said, pushing his hand into his hair.

"No," she said, gulping air past her clogged adenoids. "I'll be fine once I acclimate."

He barked out a laugh. "How long will that take?"

"I don't know," she said, bracing for a violent sneeze. From her lap she grabbed what she thought was the napkin, but wound up sneezing into the black bra. Afterward she held it up by finger and thumb and looked at Dell. "Sorry."

He grimaced and reached over to take the bra, then tossed it out his window. Then he looked at the dash, his eyes wide. "Oh, no."

"What's wrong?" she asked, squeezing the bridge of her stuffy nose.

"The engine light is on—I think it's overheated." He steered the SUV to the shoulder and turned off the engine. "I don't believe this."

"Turn on the heater," she mumbled.

"What? Why?"

"It'll lower the engine temperature."

He looked dubious, but he did what she suggested, then climbed out and raised the hood. Steam hissed into the air. Dell waved his arms back and forth, looking for the source.

"Check the radiator cap for a leak," she called, then blew her nose heartily.

"Yeowww!" he howled.

She sighed, then grabbed the jock strap and climbed out to find Dell holding his burnt fingers. "It's hot," she added.

"I knew that," he said, swearing and waving his red fingers in the air. "I just forgot."

"Stand back," she said, then used the jock strap to loosen the cap. No radiator fluid spewed out, only more steam. She leaned in and poked at the radiator hoses, zeroing in on a hole the size of a pencil eraser. "There's your problem—a burst hose."

He looked at her, his expression incredulous. "You know about cars?"

She frowned. "A little. Do you have an extra hose?"

"No."

"Radiator fluid?"

He sighed. "No."

"Wait here." Gabrielle walked to the back of the SUV, sneezing three times in a row and dabbing at her eyes. She opened the hatch and rummaged through her backpack, removing a roll of black electrical tape, a bottle of water, a tube of burn salve and a white bandage. She walked back to the front. "Let me see your hand."

He worked his mouth from side to side, then reluctantly turned over his wounded hand for her inspection. Angry raised blisters formed a line across the underside of his large fingers. She made a rueful noise then opened the bottle of water and, holding his big hand steady, poured cool water over the violated skin. He sucked in a breath, then exhaled in relief.

Gabrielle's own breathing seemed to be compromised, too, and she couldn't blame it entirely on her allergies. Watching the water splash over their hands seemed more erotic than simple first aid. Tamping down her visceral reaction to him, she squeezed the burn salve onto her fingertips and applied it to the blisters as carefully as possible. He winced, but he didn't complain. With her hands shaking, she tore open the bandage and wrapped it around his fingers twice before securing the end.

"There," she said cheerfully. But when she looked up, she was caught up in his deep, brown eyes that reflected surprise and…desire? She realized that they were standing close enough for her to see the little nicks where he'd cut himself shaving this morning. Instead of his usual designer cologne, the scent of strong soap emanated from his skin. Everything about him was so male, and called to all those things in her that were female.

He wet his lips, and she knew he could sense the pheromones he'd stirred in her body. He leaned in until their lips were mere inches apart. "What now?" he murmured. "We seem to be…stranded."

At the brush of his breath against her mouth, panic shot through her stomach. Certainly he didn't intend to *kiss* her. Maybe she had something in her eye…a leaf in her hair… Yet he seemed to be looking at her mouth, and wasn't this just how she'd always fantasized it would be between her and Dell? That he would look into her eyes and fall in love with her? That he would kiss her and realize she was the one?

Her breasts grew heavy and she forgot to breathe until her lungs contracted and she had to gasp for air. The shock to her system jarred her back to reality and into motion. "Stranded?" she said, turning back to the exposed engine. "Not necessarily."

With renewed focus, she used her teeth to tear off a foot-long piece of the black electrical tape and reached in to tightly wrap the damaged hose. Retrieving the bottle of water, she said, "Stand back."

He did, watching intently. She carefully poured the rest of the water into the radiator, pulling back until the steam slowed, then replaced the cap loosely. "Start it up," she said.

Looking doubtful, he climbed in and started the engine. She checked to make sure the hose was holding and left the radiator cap loose in case pressure built up again, then lowered the hood and wiped her hands on her pants.

She climbed back inside and settled into her seat, trying to put their close encounter out of her mind. "Drive slowly to the next service station." She blew her nose again—the brief time outside had sent her allergies into overdrive.

"Thanks," Dell said. "That was…impressive."

"Next time you might want to put as much thought into a roadside repair kit as you do your makeout kit," she mumbled, stuffing the condoms and body lube back into the glove compartment, and pulling out another wad of paper napkins. Her foggy head was making her bold, she realized, and she hoped the flush on her cheeks could be attributed to the heat. With everything at stake, she couldn't believe that she'd almost succumbed to his indiscriminate sex appeal.

And worse…how utterly lame was it that she knew more about how to fix a radiator hose than how to put on a condom?

DELL STARED at the slip of a woman slumped in the passenger seat, carsick, her nose and eyes red from unseen allergens. She'd just saved their asses…and had given him the best—or should he say worst—hard-on in recent memory.

What other surprises did Gabby have up her prim little sleeve?

He pulled back onto the road and drove slowly, keeping an eye out for the engine light to come back on. Soft snores sounded and he looked over to see Gabby's mouth slack in sleep, her face a becoming shade of pink. The allergy attack must have zapped her, he realized, still marveling over her ingenuity and feeling a little upstaged by her preparedness.

A tiny blip of alarm zigzagged through his chest. Was this a foreboding of how the competition would play out?

Then he laughed at his own musings. A road repair that she'd learned in a women's magazine article was one thing, but surviving in the elements was quite another. Her snoring escalated and he smirked. After all, the mere *drive* to the competition had put her under.

But it gave him a chance to study the puzzling young woman—the elegant, understated lines of her face, her long, graceful hands and feet, her slender figure and the lush curve of her breasts. In between teasing her in the hallways at the office, how had her quiet beauty escaped him all these years?

Because he typically went for the obvious

beauties, like Courtney, he realized. Because he knew what to expect from women like Courtney-fun and fleeting involvement, with no strings. But a quiet little bird like Gabby was likely inexperienced with relationships and would probably misconstrue sex with something crazy, like *love*.

Dell flexed his bandaged hand. He did not need the complication of love in his life, not when his career was bulleting up and he already had less free time than he'd like to pursue the outdoor sports he enjoyed.

He forced his attention from the slender beauty back to the road. For the meantime, he'd stick to the obvious.

A few miles later, he pulled into a mom-and-pop service station and still Gabby didn't awaken. He introduced himself to a skinny young guy named Walt who wore overalls over a shirtless, bony chest. "Can you replace a radiator hose?"

The man spat in the dirt. "No problem. Pull 'er in."

Dell pulled the SUV into the place the man indicated, frowning when he saw the guy staring at Gabby through the window.

"Pretty girl," Walt said when Dell climbed out to oversee the work. "Daughter?"

"No," Dell said sharply. Christ, did she look that young, and he that old? "Girlfriend," he felt compelled to add firmly, to divert the man's attention.

Walt grunted and lifted the hood. "Hmm, nice repair job."

"Thanks," Dell said, further rankled.

"This'll take me a few minutes." Walt stopped and wrote something on a slip. "Take this to the cashier and she'll ring you up."

Dell opened the driver-side door to crack the windows in the SUV, his glance landing on Gabby's heart-shaped face, flushed from the heat, long, golden lashes resting on high cheekbones, surrounded by curls that had sprung loose from her ponytail in the humidity. She did look more like a teenager than a woman he should be lusting after, but the swell of her breasts beneath her T-shirt and the memory of her breathless arousal when they had almost kissed under the hood proved that she was every ounce a woman.

A woman smart enough not to let him kiss her.

He frowned and locked the doors of the SUV, then walked into the area where sundries were sold to pay the cashier for the repair. While he was there, he bought a package of allergy medicine and a bottle of water for Gabby. By the time he returned, Walt was lowering the hood.

"Start her up," he directed Dell.

Gabby stirred when he started the engine, but didn't fully waken until he pulled from the uneven paved lot back onto the road.

"Where are we?" she asked, sitting up and rubbing her eyes.

"I just had the radiator hose replaced, not too far from where we broke down." He offered her a smile and nodded at the bag and bottle of water on the seat between them. "I got you some allergy medicine," he said, feeling strangely proud of himself.

"Thank you," she murmured, reaching for the bag. "Are we almost there?"

"No," he said, glancing at his watch with a frown. "Is there a number on those papers where I can call ahead to tell them we're going to be late?" Then he glanced at his cell phone and muttered a curse under his breath. "Never mind, there's no cell service here."

She pushed one of the capsules through the blister pack and popped it in her mouth, chasing it with a drink from the bottle. "How late are we going to be?"

"A couple of hours, at least." Which would not be the best impression to make on Eddie Fosser from CEG.

She grabbed her stomach as they rounded a curve. "Ooh, slow down." She rolled down the window, then sneezed mightily, twice.

He sighed and eased off the gas, settling in for a painstakingly slow drive up the mountain to their destination. Gabby alternately dozed and sneezed and moaned. Obviously the medicine hadn't kicked in yet. He was tempted to turn around and take her back to Atlanta and tuck her into bed.

His bed.

Dell frowned. It seemed…*unnatural* to feel horny and protective at the same time. The altitude must be affecting him, he decided, working his jaw to get his ears to pop and release pent-up pressure.

If only it were that easy to release pressure building in other parts of his body.

As they crept along, the scenery, at least, was spectacular—the sloping fields lush with tall grass and lined with thick trees. In the distance, foot-hills of the rugged Georgia Mountains loomed, which included the approach paths for the Appa-lachian Trail.

After what seemed like an eternity of driving, Gabby pointed to a sign. "There's the place we're going—the Clay Stream Trail, five miles."

Dell sighed in relief. "Five miles. Great."

Ominous clouds were gathering on the horizon, prompting him to hope that they arrived before the threatened rain set in.

Suddenly, the engine sputtered, then died. Dell thumped the steering wheel. "Not again."

Gabby sat up and leaned over. "I don't think it's

your radiator this time," she said, her voice nasally from the allergies.

Her superior tone irritated him to no end. "Why not?"

"Because the 'fuel empty' light is on. We're out of gas."

6

DELL STARED at the little light on the dashboard that read "Fuel empty," incredulous that he'd been so careless as to run out of gas. Where was his head?

Gabby's laughter rang out, and he looked over to concede wryly that his head had been wrapped around *this* redhead since their confrontation in Bruce's office. The expression of delight on her face—her flashing green eyes, her wide smile—would have made his day except for the fact that it was at his expense. "I don't see what's so funny."

"Then you're not looking," she said simply, opening the door and sliding out of sight. "We'd better start walking if we're going to make it to camp."

"But it's five miles!"

She reappeared in the open door and gestured to the deserted mountain road. "When was the last time a car passed us? And it's way more than five miles back to that station. I say let's walk toward the camp. If a car comes along, we can always flag it down."

She closed the door and walked to the rear of the SUV.

He climbed out, closing his door with a bang. "What are you doing?"

"Getting my backpack."

He scoffed. "You can't carry that thing for five miles." Her smile evaporated and he immediately missed it.

"Watch me." She pulled the pack to the edge, then turned around and shrugged into the shoulder harness.

"Wait," he said, seeing she was determined. "How about we swap packs?"

"No way," she said, fastening the straps across her chest, then slowly pushed to her feet. She wobbled and Dell rushed forward to steady her.

"I'm fine," she said, gaining her footing. She aimed her body uphill. "Let's go."

He sighed, but grabbed his own pack, locked the vehicle and followed her. His hand was starting to throb, but at least it kept his mind off other parts of his body that seemed to be in a bind.

They fell into a steady rhythm, and her stride impressed him, considering her size, her load and the fact that she was breathing through her mouth in deference, he assumed, to her stuffy nose. He decided that conversation would only slow her down…besides, Gabby seemed to prefer the quiet, as opposed to every other woman he knew who assumed that silence was an indication that something was wrong. It was rather refreshing…yet disconcerting at the same time.

He didn't like the fact that he was finding more things about Gabby to appreciate.

They had walked about a mile when Dell inhaled a deep breath of mountain air, which included a whiff of Gabby's fruity scent, and acknowledged, "This isn't so bad."

The words had barely left his mouth when the first raindrop fell on his cheek. Before he could reach up to wipe it away, a downpour had descended.

He expected Gabby to squeal and flail about, but to his amazement, she raised her face to the sky and stuck out her tongue to catch a few raindrops before reaching around to unhook a lightweight jacket from her backpack. She threw the hooded jacket over her head and shoulders, shielding herself from the rain, which began to pummel them in earnest. Realizing it was foolish to push on, Dell grabbed her hand.

"Come on," he urged, and ran toward a cluster of trees alongside the road. They huddled under the canopy of an enormous oak tree to escape the torrent.

"It probably won't last too long," he said, shivering because he was soaked through to his underwear.

"Do you have something to dry off with?" Gabby asked, shaking her raincoat.

He opened his dripping backpack for a look

inside—a couple of changes of underwear, a pair of thick socks, a pair of swim trunks, two T-shirts and a stick of deodorant. He set the pack aside. "No need, I'm fine."

Gabby unfastened her backpack and dropped it to the ground. From an outside pocket she retrieved a small towel and proceeded to wipe her face and arms. Afterward, she offered it to him, but he stubbornly refused.

"How much stuff did you pack?" he asked with a laugh.

She shrugged. "Enough to get through a weekend in the wilderness, like the papers said."

He bit down on the inside of his jaw, fighting the nagging sensation of panic that he hadn't thoroughly read the papers Bruce had given him. He'd assumed that CEG would be providing all the equipment they needed. Besides clothes and deodorant, he'd brought only a bedroll, which was now thoroughly soaked.

Like him. He suppressed a shiver, and sank down to join Gabby leaning against the tree trunk.

"Do you think they'll send someone to look for us?" she asked.

"I hope not. Getting waylaid before I even make it to the site isn't the impression I want to make on Eddie Fosser."

She frowned. "What about me?"

He didn't say anything, only shifted, trying to find a more comfortable position against the tree.

"It doesn't matter what impression he has of me, does it?" she asked.

"I didn't say that."

"But you were thinking it."

"I was thinking that this is a competition," he said, flustered as much by the lose-lose direction of the conversation as much as the proximity of a rain-scented Gabby.

"Yes, it is," she murmured, locking gazes with him, her eyes brimming with determination.

Tendrils of red-gold hair formed damp ringlets around her hairline, and the sprinkling of freckles across her nose and cheeks seemed to stand out in relief on her dewy skin. Her long lashes were dark and spiky with wetness, her lips full and ripe. Her sexy youthfulness seemed all the more potent against the backdrop of a summer rainstorm that had them sequestered under the shelter of an ancient tree. Her damp T-shirt was molded to her body, outlining her breasts and her budded nipples.

A shudder of desire rippled through him, triggering another wave of shivering as gooseflesh raised on his wet arms. His shoulder brushed hers.

"I have a sweatshirt you can borrow," she murmured.

"I'm okay," he insisted.

Except he wasn't okay. Sitting next to her in a cocoon of humidity, he was overcome with the urge to kiss her hard and well, to feel her mouth and body expand under him. She must have sensed his intention because the tip of her tongue flicked out to moisten her pink lower lip.

Dell took it as an invitation and before he could analyze the implication, he leaned forward and captured her sweet mouth with his, gratified when her gasp of surprise gave way to a passionate kiss whose intensity surprised even him.

Her tongue speared into his mouth, her teeth clicked against his and she angled her face for better access to him. Her enthusiasm caught him off guard, and sent white-hot longing to swell his sex. He reached up to cup one luscious breast, and nearly came undone as his thumb closed over a stiff nipple.

But suddenly Gabby withdrew. "Dell…"

"Don't stop," he murmured, nipping at her swollen mouth.

"I hear a car," she said, pushing him away and lunging to her feet. She grabbed her raincoat and pack and ran through the pouring rain to the side of the road, waving her free arm at the approaching pickup truck. "Hey! We need help!"

The pickup stopped and the driver rolled down his window. To Dell's chagrin, it was Walt, the young man from the service station who had replaced the radiator hose, grinning at Gabby in her wet T-shirt as if she were a gift that had dropped out of the sky with the rain.

Dell frowned, picked up his pack and jogged through the rain, thinking that at least the dousing would cool his libido. He sidled up next to Gabby. Walt's smile diminished a bit, but he waved them into the cab of his dilapidated truck.

"Get in," he shouted through the rain.

Dell yanked open the door to find an enormous white dog lying in the middle of the bench seat.

"Throw your packs in the back," Walt said. "You and your girlfriend will have to double up."

"I'm not his—*ow!*"

Dell didn't regret pinching Gabby on the behind, although from the sharp look she gave him, he realized he should think twice—or at least get permission—before trying it again.

"Thanks, man," he said, then threw their backpacks into the rusty truck bed that had a missing tailgate. He urged Gabby to climb inside. He followed her and slammed the door closed, then pulled her onto his lap. She resisted at first, then balanced her shapely rear cautiously on his leg, with one hand on the dash and one hand on the back of the seat. He gave her a wry look, thinking she was acting mighty prim for someone who'd just kissed him with so much voltage his clothes had almost dried out.

The jacket Gabby had held over her head and shoulders hadn't offered her much protection this time. Water dripped from her ponytail, her nose and her chin. Her clothes were vacuumed to her body, highlighting every delicious detail. He wished he had a blanket to toss over her to stop her shivering…and to hide her from Walt's prying gaze.

The truck was a stick shift and had no shocks to speak of. The only advantage was that Gabby bounced around, breasts jiggling, finally landing squarely in his lap. She stiffened, then wriggled against him. He leaned forward and whispered in her ear, "Be still—you're only making it worse."

She froze and he willed away the throbbing erection, but with Gabby pressed against him, and the sway of the truck from side to side, it was impossible not to be aware of her. Walt hit a pothole that bounced her so high her head almost hit the roof of the cab. When she came back down, the impact on his privates nearly took Dell's breath away.

"Sorry," she whispered.

"It's okay," he managed.

Meanwhile the stench of wet dog and wet bodies in such a confined space with no air conditioner was overwhelming. When Walt wheeled onto the side road that took them the last few hundred yards to their destination, the rain finally slackened. Then as abruptly as it had started, the rain stopped.

"Finally," Dell muttered as they pulled into a clearing where a small building sat.

"This it?" Walt asked.

Gabby was referencing soggy papers she'd pulled out of one of the pockets in her cargo pants. "Clay Stream Trail. This is it."

Before the truck had rolled to a complete stop, Dell had opened the door to usher in some blessed fresh air. Gabby scrambled down from his lap, inflicting more damage, but he ground his jaw until she had slid to the ground. He climbed out gingerly, then reached for his wallet and withdrew a twenty to extend to their driver.

But the man wasn't paying attention because he was mesmerized by the sight of Gabby in her transparent T-shirt, shaking the moisture from her lightweight jacket. Her full breasts were perfectly outlined, with the rings of her rigid nipples as clear as if she were nude. Dell's throat convulsed, then he looked back to Walt, frowned and waved the money. "For your trouble," he said.

The man took the money and grinned. "Weren't no trouble, mister. You sure are a lucky man."

Dell gave the man a sour look. "Thanks. Here's another hundred if you'll get my SUV gassed up and leave it here for me before Monday morning."

The man nodded and took the hundred. "Will do."

Dell handed him the keys, then reached Gabby

in two strides and leaned in close to her ear. "You should put your jacket back on."

"I'm not cold."

He poked his tongue into his cheek and nodded to the twin peaks of her breasts. "I beg to differ."

She looked down and gasped, then tried to cover herself while she yanked on her jacket.

With great effort, Dell averted his gaze and lifted her backpack from the truck bed. Then he frowned. "Where's my pack?"

Gabby looked up. "I don't know."

Walt stuck his head out. "Must have bounced out when I hit that big crater of a pothole way back yonder. I'll look for it when I go back for your SUV, but it's probably roadkill by now."

Dell closed his eyes and counted to ten. When he opened them, Gabby was fighting a smile.

"I brought plenty of supplies," she said. "We can share."

"No, thanks," he said stiffly, then gestured toward the building. "I'm sure they sell supplies at this outpost. I should be able to throw together what I need."

She shrugged. "Suit yourself."

Walt honked his horn as he drove away and Dell gave a wry wave, then turned to follow Gabby toward the building. The memory of her surprising kiss and her behind grinding against his lap for the past five miles still made it difficult to walk comfortably.

The door to the building opened and Eddie Fosser, president of CEG, emerged. His big, stocky build reminded Dell of a middle-aged linebacker with an amiable smile. He walked past Gabby and extended his hand to Dell.

"Dell, we were about to send a search party out to look for you."

Dell shook the man's hand. "Sorry, Eddie, I had a little engine trouble, and we had to catch a ride. Tried to call, but my phone's not working up here."

"Mine, either. Most peace and quiet I've had in years. What happened to your hand?"

"Uh, long story."

"Did you bring Miss Flannery with you?"

Dell looked back to Gabby, feeling a foreign pang—sympathy?—that Fosser had walked right by her.

"I'm Gabrielle Flannery, Mr. Fosser," she said, stepping up to extend her hand. With her wet ponytail and big, green eyes, she looked like a gangly slip of a girl who weighed about as much as one of Fosser's legs.

"Nice to meet you, Miss Flannery."

She smiled. "We've met a couple of times, sir, when I was at CEG with Courtney Rodgers for presentations."

Which meant, Dell knew, that she'd run the projector while Courtney talked, or passed out donuts or something inconsequential. He knew, because he'd done the same thing to assistants on his own accounts. Dell squirmed while Fosser searched his mind, then recovered.

"Oh, yes, of course, I remember. Good to see you again. And I understand that you're competing with Dell to handle my account."

"Yes, sir."

He looked back to Dell, his eyes wide with barely disguised amusement. Dell could feel the man telegraphing, *You've got to be kidding.* It was, Dell agreed, going to be a very lopsided competition. He'd have to do what he could to keep from embarrassing Gabby too much.

Eddie clapped his hands. "Okay, let's go inside and meet everyone so we can get this show on the road." He gestured to the impressive-looking backpack leaned against a post. "Grab your backpack, Dell. I see you have our top-of-line model. Very nice."

"Oh, that's mine," Gabby said, hefting it by its handle.

Eddie's eyebrows climbed, then he frowned at Dell's empty hands. "Where's your pack?"

"Another long story," Dell muttered.

"No matter," Eddie said with a mock punch to

Dell's shoulder. "You're such an outdoorsman, I'm sure you'll be fine."

Dell tried to return the man's smile, but didn't miss Gabby's worried glance at the man's blatant favoritism.

They walked into the small wood building that was lined with souvenirs and T-shirts, then continued through to a room built onto the back that was stocked with generic rental equipment.

A group of eight people stood, their attention riveted on the blond, tanned movie star Nick Ocean, who was telling an animated story. His perfect Clorox smile was set off by a white golf shirt with turned-up collar, his expensive designer sunglasses perched on the top of his head. Nearby a photographer with a professional-looking camera snapped shots of Nick. They arrived just as he delivered a punch line, because the group erupted into laughter, one woman's high-pitched giggle overriding everyone else's as she reached forward to touch the man's arm suggestively.

Dell winced inwardly. Lynda Gilbert, CEG public relations. The brunette was predatory, and had tried to ensnare him once at a conference. Lynda had been tempting, but something about her had made him think twice and, ultimately, decline her sultry invitation. He glanced around the rest of the group, but the faces were unfamiliar.

"Here are our last guests," Eddie Fosser announced. "Dell Kingston and Gabrielle Flannery from Noble Marketing in Atlanta." He went around the room making introductions.

"This is my executive assistant, Elliot Borders," he said, indicating a slight, thin bespectacled man whose eyes were whip-smart, but looked as if he'd never spent a day outdoors.

"And Wally Moon, buyer for Price Land, one of our biggest customers." Wally Moon was a clean-cut, frat-boy type with a beer gut and a slightly arrogant tilt to his mouth.

"This is Mike Strong, a buyer for our biggest sports equipment chain, The Great Outdoors." Mike Strong was thickly muscled and stood ramrod straight, his eyes intense. He probably had a military background, Dell guessed, and looked hardcore.

"And Lynda Gilbert from CEG's public relations department," Eddie continued, nodding to the brunette.

"Dell and I have met," she cooed.

Next to him, he felt Gabby stiffen and was it his imagination, or did she inch away from him?

"And of course you know our spokesman, Nick Ocean," Eddie said with a little laugh.

Nick smiled and gave one of those blinking, "I'm a star" head nods. His eyes seemed to linger on

Gabby, whose breathing suddenly seemed compromised—and not from allergies, Dell surmised wryly.

"This is Joe, a local guide and our photographer this weekend," Eddie continued, gesturing to the artsy guy with the camera. Joe gave them a "dude" two-finger wave.

"And Karen, our equipment expert and guide," Eddie said, pointing to the sturdy, bohemian-looking woman who might have been anywhere from thirty to fifty. She gave the group a tight smile, then stepped to the front of the room.

"Okay, everyone's here to have a little competitive fun and try out some new CEG products. Throughout the weekend you'll earn points for competing in and winning both individual and group challenges. There will be a maximum of one thousand points possible, and the top challenger will go home with a great prize." She glanced around, giving everyone confirming nods, as a camp counselor would, before continuing.

"This afternoon we're going to run through a few riding and climbing drills. Tomorrow we'll have some fun on the river. And I hope you packed a good backpack like we asked because we're going to put your survival skills to the test."

Dell felt a glimmer of panic. Backpack? Damn, he really should have read those papers.

"And just so that everyone knows," Eddie Fosser

broke in, "we have a little competition within the competition going on. Dell and Gabrielle are competing to take over the CEG account at Noble Marketing." He slanted a smile in their direction, making amused eye contact with Dell. "Whichever one of them scores highest over the course of the weekend will win."

Chuckles went up from the group, and all the men grinned at him, then glanced at Gabby with sympathy.

She noticed it, too, he realized, from the anxious look that came over her face. Dammit, why did Eddie have to tell everyone?

Karen's eyes glittered sadistically as she raised a whistle to her mouth and blew it with gusto. "Let the competition begin."

Dell glanced at Gabby and she locked gazes with him, her large green eyes shining with determination, her pink mouth set in a tight bow, like when he'd first dared her to come on this trip.

Something in his chest—and pants—moved, sending a shot of lust through his body, and suddenly he was seized with an overwhelming sense of anticipation. There was no way little Gabby Flannery was going to beat him this weekend.

But it sure would be fun watching her try.

7

GABRIELLE WAS ACCUSTOMED to feeling like an outsider. But she'd never felt more out of place than now, looking over the faces of the group. They were laughing at her, feeling sorry for her because she was obviously delusional to believe she could beat Dell. Why hadn't she simply conceded to Dell when he'd given her the chance in Bruce's office? Why did he have to make that stupid dare? And why had she risen to his bait?

One magazine article, she realized, did not an expert risk-taker make.

Their guide Karen directed them outside to a shelter where a light lunch had been set up. While the others filed outside, Gabrielle asked her if there was a place she could change clothes.

"By the T-shirts," Karen said, pointing in the direction they'd entered. "Hey, are you the same Gabrielle that I've been e-mailing product specs to for the past year?"

Gabrielle smiled. "Yes. You're that Karen?"

"Yeah. Nice to meet you." Karen stuck out her hand and Gabrielle shook it. "Good luck in the competition—you should do well."

"I'm not…that athletic."

Karen dismissed her concern with a wave. "This weekend is as much about brains as brawn." She leaned in conspiratorially. "I'll be rooting for you."

"Thanks," Gabrielle said, her confidence rising a notch. She carried her damp pack into the souvenir area and found the changing closet. A glance in the mirror made her wince—her red hair had taken on a life of its own, forming corkscrew curls where it wasn't bound. She removed the elastic band and finger-combed it as best she could. Then she peeled the wet clothes from her clammy body, longing for a hot shower. She used a hand towel from her backpack to rub her skin until it tingled.

She smiled wryly, remembering when she was a kid, trying to rub off the freckles that sprinkled her arms and nose. Another glance in the mirror put a blush on her cheeks when she remembered Dell's kiss…the way he'd touched her breast…how transparent her T-shirt had been when they'd arrived. How he had seemed…aroused. And his erection when she'd sat on his lap had been impossible to ignore, pressing against her bottom, with only a few layers of clothing separating their erogenous zones. Just the memory of it made her womb contract with desire. And she wondered where that kiss would've led if it hadn't been interrupted, what it would feel like to have Dell make love to her. She'd thought about it before—many times—but before she hadn't had the knowledge of a kiss to fuel her fantasies.

Suddenly, the door opened and Dell squeezed in sideways, whistling under his breath. Her gasp coincided with the sound of the door slamming shut behind him. His eyes flew wide and he held up his hands, dropping the clothes he'd brought in. For a few seconds, they both seemed paralyzed.

"I didn't know anyone was—" His voice cut off as he unabashedly stared at her body.

She scrambled to cover her nude self with a hand towel, her heart thrashing wildly. Had she unconsciously left the door unlocked, had she somehow willed him to come inside with her wayward thoughts of lovemaking?

"I—" His Adam's apple bobbed. "I…God, Gabby…you're…*gorgeous.*"

Get out, her mind screamed, but the familiar wordlessness seized her as her thoughts reeled and alien feelings took root in her chest…feminine pride?

"Dell?" A voice sounded from the other side of the door.

Gabrielle recognized it as Lynda Gilbert—the woman who had seemed to "know" Dell—and froze.

Instead of answering, Dell silently reached behind him and turned the lock on the door, raising a finger to his lips for her not to give him— them—away.

A tremor ran through her at the surreal experience of having Dell see her nude...her mind told her it was wrong, but her body didn't seem to care. In fact, it seemed...natural.

His deep brown eyes shone with a hunger that made her bare breasts ache. She knew she should tell him to leave, but she couldn't form the words. Her skin felt scorched under his gaze, her chest rising and falling with short, shallow breaths.

The woman rattled the doorknob. "Dell, are you in there?"

Ignoring the other woman, Dell stepped closer and clasped her arms, then lowered his mouth to her neck, trailing hot, wet kisses up to her ear.

"N-no, he isn't," Gabrielle said loudly, rolling her shoulders against the waves of pleasure that broke over her body. The flimsy hand towel fell to the floor. "It's me...Gabrielle."

He exhaled thickly at her state of total nudity, then trailed a finger back and forth over the curve of her collarbone, raising gooseflesh in anticipation of him touching her bare breasts. And when he seemed in no hurry to fulfill her fantasy, she took his hands and placed them there.

His sigh in her ear mirrored the gasp of pleasure that lodged in her throat at the feel of his warm hands palming her breasts, sending ribbons of longing unfurling in her limbs.

"Have you seen Dell?" Lynda called.

Nuzzling her neck, he massaged her breasts, tugging on her nipples. The rough scrape of his bandage felt erotic against her tender skin.

"N-no," she said for the woman's sake.

He captured her mouth in a searing kiss, wrapping his arms around her. Then he cupped her bare bottom and pulled her against the erection evident even through his clothes.

"Are you sure?" the woman called.

He leaned down and took one stiff nipple into his mouth. Gabrielle pressed her fist against her mouth to keep from crying out as he drew on her greedily. "Yes," she said, both to the woman and in response to Dell. The shock of seeing his mouth on her breast sent a rush of moisture to the juncture of her thighs, and her knees nearly buckled. He caught her, and cupped his hand over the nest of curls between her thighs.

"If you see him," the woman called, "tell him that Lynda is looking for him."

Gabrielle stiffened, and her eyes flew open. How many times had Dell and Lynda engaged in this kind of behavior? Making out in a semipublic place? Humiliation rolled over her as she remembered Tori's words that the entire office thought Dell was going to get into her pants. She'd spent a mere half day with Dell and he'd already seen her naked…and more.

Dell must have detected her withdrawal because he slowly pulled away from her, then dragged his hand down his face as the woman's footsteps faded away. "I'm sorry, Gabby. I lost my head," he murmured, visibly trying to compose himself. "It's just that you look—" He averted his gaze and sighed. "Why don't you finish getting dressed, and slip out? I'll wait and follow in a few minutes."

She nodded, unable to respond. She couldn't be angry, couldn't say she hadn't enjoyed what had happened. Her body still pulsed from his hands and mouth. She could have stopped him, but she hadn't. The adrenaline rush had turned her mind to pulp— anything that robbed a person of their ability to think had to be a bad thing.

She turned her back to him and closed her eyes in self-reproach. After the initial shock had dissipated, she'd wanted him to touch her, wanted to know what it felt like to be made love to by a man like Dell instead of the few fumbling boyfriends she'd known. She yanked dry clothes from her bag and began to dress as quickly as she could.

What must he think of her?

DELL THOUGHT he might come undone.

With Herculean effort, he dragged his gaze away from Gabby's stunningly lush body, only to find the back of her reflected in the mirror on the door. His stiff cock pulsed at the sight of the indention of her spine, her finely tapered waist, the unexpected flare of her hips and the most shapely behind he'd ever seen. He reached down to adjust his aching erection, and wished like hell that he could satisfy his lust for Gabby right then and there. But it would be wrong considering the situation, and unfair to Gabby to take her standing up in a changing room, as if they were a couple of teenagers.

He closed his eyes to her reflection—not that it did much good, since all of her was now branded onto this brain. But he kept his eyes closed, listening to the rustling sounds of her dressing, inhaling that fruity fragrance she wore, the taste of her sweet skin still on his lips.

Remorse coursed through him—he'd seen the look in her eyes of surprise and surrender. Making out in a changing room wasn't the sort of thing that Gabby did…but perhaps she had fantasized about it?

Maybe had even fantasized about it with him?

He set his jaw against the latent desire that throbbed in his body. This couldn't happen again…the last thing he needed was for Gabby to fall for him…that would make working at Noble way too uncomfortable…and working with her on the CEG account nearly impossible.

He glanced up when she left the changing room, and the look of nervous regret in her eyes hammered the idea home that the two of them hooking up would solve one of his immediate problems—the fact that his lust for her had hijacked his concentration.

But it would create so many more.

The bottom line was that he didn't want to deal with the aftermath of an emotionally attached Gabby…and, he realized with a start, he didn't want Gabby to be hurt.

He undressed quickly and frowned at the garish T-shirt and swim trunks he'd pulled from the racks of the souvenir shop.

The door swung open and Dell looked up to see Lynda Gilbert standing there, staring at his cock as if she were ready to pounce. "There you are," she said, her red mouth curling.

Dell covered his privates and gave her a tight smile. "Just trying to get into some dry clothes."

Her eyes glittered provocatively. "Need some help?"

Dell glanced over her "obvious" package—the makeup, the perfectly arranged hair, the form-fitting and color coordinated clothing—and couldn't help but compare it to Gabby's natural beauty and understated sexuality. His erection shrank.

"No, thanks—I think I got it."

"Okay," the woman said with a pouty, dramatic sigh. "We'll catch up later—after a little while in the woods, I'm sure we'll both be looking for something to entertain ourselves."

She raked her gaze over him again, then closed the door. Dell expelled a noisy sigh and hurriedly dressed in the yellow T-shirt emblazoned with Rappellers Do It In The Air, and a pair of black swim trunks with a set of bright orange handprints on the ass. With his wet hiking boots, he looked like a bona fide idiot.

He emerged from the dressing room and bought a stick of deodorant and a couple of other T-shirts to shove into a fluorescent backpack that looked more like a grade-school bookbag than a piece of outdoor equipment. Feeling irritable, he exited to the shelter, where everyone sat eating.

His gaze immediately sought out Gabby, and he found her, eating a sandwich and talking to Nick Ocean. With a frown, Dell noted that the man's body language was decidedly flirtatious.

Suddenly not that hungry, Dell grabbed a protein bar and a bottle of water and headed over to see what kind of bull the guy was spewing.

"Hello," Dell said smoothly when he walked up

to the couple. Gabby suddenly seemed fascinated with finishing her sandwich.

"Hi," Nick said in his radio announcer voice. "Dave, right?"

"Dell."

"Right," Nick said amiably. "You and Gabby work together."

An unreasonable streak of jealousy raced through Dell—he was the only one who called her "Gabby." "That's right, Gabrielle and I work together." He turned to Gabby and tried to behave as if he didn't know what lay beneath that baggy gray T-shirt. "How are your allergies?"

Her eye contact was fleeting. "I'm fine."

"You certainly look fine to me," Nick said, giving her a ten-thousand-dollar smile.

A blush bloomed on her cheeks. "Rain usually settles the pollen in the air."

Another irrational pang of jealousy stabbed Dell—he'd been making Gabby blush for years now. Who did this guy think he was?

"Nick was just telling me about the movie he wrapped in Brazil," Gabby said.

Dell frowned. Oh, right—the guy was a movie star. "Do you perform your own stunts?" he asked the man.

Nick made a rueful noise. "I'd like to, but my contracts forbid it—the insurance alone would bankrupt the production companies. Nice T-shirt, Dave."

"It's *Dell*," he said, poking his tongue into his cheek.

The piercing sound of a whistle split the air. "Time to head over to the obstacle course, everyone," Karen announced. "Follow me."

She led the way down a short trail to a clearing the size of a football field. A fifteen-foot climbing wall had been constructed in the center, with a rappelling wall on the other side, and other obstacles dotted the field, including a rope swinging over a water trap, balance beams and monkey bars. Around the perimeter was a dirt and gravel track with manmade hills, divots and ramps, perfect for mountain bike riding. Indeed, lined up at the end of the track were brand new CEG mountain bikes and helmets.

"I'm going to have you divide into two teams to compete in the obstacle course," Karen announced. "The obstacle course will test athletic ability, and how you utilize CEG equipment." She gave the group a smile. "Since Dell and Gabrielle are competing against each other this weekend, I'll make them team captains. Gabrielle, go ahead and pick your first team member."

Gabrielle hesitated, glancing over the group.

Choose Eddie, Dell urged her silently. *Go for the boss.*

"I choose Elliot," she said, opting for Eddie's slight and very probably gay executive assistant.

Dell winced inwardly for her. "I choose Eddie."

Gabrielle pointed to the chubby buyer for the large retail chain. "Wally."

Ooh, another bad choice. Dell nodded to the big, beefy buyer for the outdoor store chain. "Mike."

"Nick," Gabrielle said, much to Dell's chagrin.

"Lynda," he said, trying to sound cheerful in light of the fact that Nick was already high-fiving Gabby, and he was stuck with Lynda, who squealed and gave him a full-body hug when she ran up to join his "team."

Karen walked them through the obstacle course, taking time to demonstrate the climbing and rappelling equipment. Dell zoned out—he knew all that stuff like the back of his hand. He was more interested in the fact that Nick Ocean seemed to be hovering around Gabby, touching her arm or waist for no discernible reason. When everyone else did a practice run, he waived his turn, more concerned with watching Gabby's anxious expression when she scaled the climbing wall at a snail's pace and rappelled jerkily down the wall on the other side. She was, he realized, afraid of heights.

But she didn't complain or whine, she simply pushed through the practice run in spite of her phobia, which was apparent to him. He felt a pang of sympathy for her—she was so out of her element, slathering on sunscreen every spare moment. But she put on a brave face, offering words of encouragement to her teammates as they struggled through the practice run.

His team, on the other hand, was bored. Mike and Eddie held beers from an unknown source, and Lynda had found a spot to sun herself, pulling up her top to expose her midriff and arching her body to its best advantage.

Karen called them to gather around for a navigation demonstration with CEG's newest models of compasses and handheld global positioning devices. Then she gave a rundown of CEG's latest mountain bike, the Thundertrail, and gave them all a chance to select a bike and ride it around. Since he'd logged over five hundred miles on his own mountain bike this year, Dell used the time to try to get a signal on his phone to check messages, to no avail. When he put away his phone he realized that everyone except him was wearing padded biking pants—probably a directive in the "papers" that he'd missed. But he'd be okay, his nuts could take a few jolts.

Hadn't Gabby had them in a vise for hours now?

The members of Gabby's team—Elliot, Nick and Wally—seemed already to be forming bonds. All the men gravitated to Gabby, of course.

The members of his team—Eddie, Mike and Lynda—seemed as if they were ready for a massage.

Finally, Karen explained the obstacle course—it would be a relay event, with one person from each team competing at a time: go once around the track on the mountain bike, then across the obstacle course in the field. Points would be lost if a person didn't complete a part of the course.

"The team captains will bring up the rear," Karen said, glancing at Dell, then Gabby.

Gabby was reading what looked like a handful of pages torn from a magazine, now wrinkled and limp. He smiled wryly—so typical that she'd be trying to squeeze in some reading over a wilderness weekend.

"Ready?" Karen asked. "Everyone in their places."

Dell watched as Elliot and Eddie climbed on the bikes and prepared to begin. Dell almost couldn't bear to watch—this would be the most lopsided competition ever witnessed.

Just like his and Gabby's competition, he mused.

But when Karen blew the whistle, Elliot outpaced Eddie in the bike competition—too late, Dell spotted Elliot's powerfully-developed thighs and realized he was a cyclist. But Eddie closed the gap during the obstacle course, and when Mike and Wally took off, Dell's team was only slightly behind.

But apparently Mike had had a little too much to drink—he was shaky swinging over the water trap and erratic on the monkey bars, but walking the balance beam proved to be his downfall. After tumbling off twice, Mike skipped it and went on to the climbing wall, where he was able to almost catch Wally.

When Lynda and Nick took off, everyone was cheering loudly, and Dell tried not to notice how Gabby yelled for Nick like a lovestruck groupie. Meanwhile, Lynda ran like a girl, and after swinging over the water trap, stopped to analyze a broken nail, losing precious time.

By the time he and Gabby took off, Dell's team was way behind. Gabby had almost finished the biking section when he got started. Dell attacked the course, wincing in pain when his balls came down hard on the seat, his feet slipping off the pedals because he was so used to being clipped in. The integrated shifting-and-braking system also threw him for a few minutes—damn, he should've listened when Karen had reviewed the new features. And his bandaged hand was on fire with pain.

He kept his eyes on Gabby ahead of him—she had swung over the water trap with graceful ease, and made her way across the monkey bars with surprising agility, but he knew he could catch her at the climbing wall.

But she surprised him, using the hand- and footholds to climb up the wall twice as fast as she'd done before. Still, he caught up with her at the top and winked at her. Once he got into the rappelling harness, he could descend in a matter of seconds. But the harness was unlike any he'd used before, and when he finally settled in, he pitched forward and was suddenly swinging upside down. Another equipment snafu on his part. Below him, Gabby reached the ground, shrugged out of her harness and bounded for the finish line.

Muttering a curse, Dell righted himself and adjusted the harness, then whizzed to the ground. He took off after Gabby, realizing with a tiny pang that he could easily overtake her, even in his soggy hiking boots. A part of him wanted to slow down, to let her win this one. But the competitive part of him won out as adrenaline surged to push him forward.

Except he hadn't counted on tripping over his shoelace. Dell went down hard, landing on his injured hand and biting dirt. By the time he'd pushed himself up from the ground, Gabby's team was celebrating. In fact, the three men hoisted her to their shoulders. With her head thrown back and her face radiant with a wide smile, she looked sun-kissed and gorgeous.

And victorious.

Dell stood staring at her and experienced the same burning sensation in his chest that he'd felt when she'd so expertly repaired the radiator hose, and when she'd returned his kiss so fervently and when she hadn't shied from him in the dressing room.

Maybe he'd underestimated this quiet slip of a woman.

And maybe this was going to be more of a battle than he'd ever imagined.

8

GABRIELLE FELT FLUSH with victory. When her team-mates put her down, Nick Ocean lent his body for stability to the point that she was forced to slide down the front of him, bike pants to bike pants.

"Nice," he said, and she wasn't convinced he was talking about her finish in the race. She gave a little laugh and disentangled herself from him. The man was attractive, but he emitted a slightly smarmy aura. However, she set aside her feelings to celebrate with her teammates. They were all sweaty and dirty, and rather pleased with them-selves. Nearby, Joe snapped photos, mostly of Nick hamming it up.

Dell walked up to Gabrielle and extended his hand. "Congratulations."

She put her hand in his and thought how strange to be shaking hands when less than an hour ago in the dressing room, they'd been prepared to shake the earth. "Thank you."

"Well done, Gabrielle," Eddie Fosser said,

coming over to congratulate her. Then he gave a wry laugh. "Although you wouldn't have won if Dell here hadn't tripped at the end." He slapped Dell on the back. "I trust that you'll be more dependable tomorrow, son."

The older man laughed again as he walked away, but to Gabby's ears the laugh was forced. He was irritated with Dell for losing to her. Everyone expected her to lose...especially Dell, she realized. And he didn't like it when things didn't go as planned.

Gabby crossed her arms, eager to clear the air— and her conscience. "Dell...what happened in the dressing room...that can't happen again."

He nodded briefly. "I agree."

She blinked at his hasty concession. "Okay...so we're on the same page?"

"Absolutely."

Something had changed—Dell could barely make eye contact with her. Either he'd written her off because she'd pulled away from him earlier, or he was angry about her team winning. Whatever the source of his sudden detachment, her disappointment was acute.

"Your chin is bleeding," she murmured, instinctively reaching up to touch him.

He reached up and his hand covered hers for one skipped heartbeat. When she pulled away her hand, he lifted the tail of his T-shirt and wiped his chin, giving her a glimpse of a six-pack of abs rivaling any she'd seen on a billboard. For a few seconds, her mind went completely blank. Then she saw the blood on his shirt, and leaned in for a better look at the cut on the end of his chin, about an inch long, and crusted with dirt. "You might need stitches."

"It'll be fine."

"At least it should be cleaned."

"I *said,* it'll be fine."

She blinked at his vehemence, hurt slicing through her chest. She inadvertently stumbled backward, reverting to her standard clumsiness she had managed to overcome during the obstacle course by rereading a few passages in the "Adrenaline Rush" article for moral support. Thankfully, she caught herself, tingling with embarrassment and feeling as if the dweeb had overstepped her bounds. For a few seconds, she felt her entire personality contract.

Dell looked remorseful. "Gabby, I—"

Karen's whistle split the air. "Everyone on Gabrielle's team receives one hundred points, and everyone on Dell's team receives fifty. But don't worry—there are more chances to earn points at tonight's campsite, which is where we're headed next. Let's go!"

Karen led the way back to the shelter, and Gabrielle kept her distance from Dell. Lynda Gilbert, on the other hand, fluttered around him like an exotic bird.

She wondered suddenly if Lynda and Dell had picked up in the dressing room where she and Dell had left off…it would help to explain why Dell was suddenly such a jerk—he didn't need her anymore for…*that.*

Nick Ocean fell in step next to her. "So, Gabrielle, what's all this about a competition between you and Dave?"

"It's Dell," she murmured. "And it's simple—we both want the CEG account. Our boss and Eddie Fosser decided that whichever one of us scores higher on the competition this weekend will get it."

Nick grinned. "And you're ahead."

"For now."

"Want me to break his arm?"

Her eyes flew wide, then she leaned in. "Have you been drinking?"

"God, yes," he said, then lifted his shirt to pat the flask stuck down in the waistband of his biking shorts. "Vodka. Makes all this Boy Scout crap bearable. Want a drink?"

"Er, no, thanks." Gabrielle slowed and let the man walk ahead. She was so glad when the shelter came back into view.

"Grab your packs, a snack and a bottle of water," Karen directed. "We're hiking to the base camp, about two miles away. We'll have dinner there and set up camp for the night."

"Will there be showers?" Lynda asked with a moan.

"Yes," Karen said.

"And real food?" asked Wally, rubbing his protruding stomach.

"Yes."

Gabrielle grabbed a bottle of water and retrieved her backpack from the storage area, noting that everyone seemed to have brought a fairly good-sized pack...except for Dell, of course—the small florescent one must be his, she decided with a smile.

On impulse, she checked her cell phone and was happy to see that she had a signal. She dialed Tori's number, and her friend answered on the first ring.

"Dog-Sitters-R-Us."

Gabrielle smirked. "Ha ha. How's the little man doing?"

"Eating me out of house and home. But at least when McGee's not eating, he's sleeping. It makes me think of getting one."

"A dog?"

"Or a boyfriend. They're really very similar you know. Eating, sleeping, barking at the television...licking themselves."

"Trust me," Gabrielle said. "A dog is *much* less trouble."

"Speaking of men and trouble, have you met Nick Ocean?"

"Yes."

"And? Is he totally effing gorgeous?"

Gabrielle glanced out the window where the participants mingled and saw Nick sneak a drink from his flask. "Yes, he's gorgeous."

"God, I'm so jealous! Did you get an autograph for me?"

"Not yet, but I will."

"So, how's it going with you and Dell?"

She tried to block out the image of Dell's hands on her naked body. "We, um, had our first competition today and…my team won."

"You mean you're ahead?"

"For now."

Tori whooped. "Wait until I tell everyone at the office tomorrow." Then Tori cleared her throat. "Has he put the moves on you yet?"

"N-no," Gabrielle said, trying to inject nonchalance into her voice. "Dell would never do anything that I didn't want him to do."

"Exactly. But men like Dell can convince you that you *do* want it."

Her throat convulsed. That was true—hadn't he already proved to be very…*persuasive?*

From outside, she heard Karen's whistle. "I have to go, Tori. Is everything else okay?"

"I guess," Tori said, her voice morose. "You're going to miss ushering at the Fox again tomorrow night."

"I know, but it's only temporary. I'll call you again when I can, okay? Give McGee a kiss for me." She disconnected the call and turned off her phone to save the battery. Then she maneuvered into her backpack as the others came in to retrieve theirs.

Dell had a sour look on his face when he picked up his adolescent's pack—combined with his bright clothing, he looked every inch the tourist. Gabrielle couldn't help smothering a smile.

Karen led the way to the trail on the opposite side of the shelter, away from the obstacle course, then counted heads before yelling, "Fall out!"

Elliot Borders, Eddie's executive assistant, caught up to her and leaned in conspiratorially. "You think she has a military background?"

Gabrielle smiled. "Or maybe she's a mother. Are you enjoying yourself?"

He wrinkled his nose. "Not yet. But it makes my boss happy when I do this kind of butchy stuff. How about you?"

She thought about it and nodded—in between feeling anxious over Dell and the competition, she was enjoying herself. "Yes, surprisingly. This isn't the kind of thing I normally do."

"Then you fake it well."

She smiled sheepishly. "That's only because I've studied the products. I wrote copy for the CEG Web site and brochures for the last couple of years while I assisted Courtney Rodgers on the account."

His smile flattened. "Oh, yes—Courtney."

"Did you know her?"

"Met her a couple of times. Quite the debutante, but she could be a ball-buster when she wanted to be." He frowned. "Are you sure you want this account? It's a bit…macho."

"I'm sure," she said, nodding to reinforce the idea to herself as well as to Elliot. "I have ideas to grow the distribution. CEG targets professionals and hardcore athletes, but I think the company is missing out on peripheral customers, like casual athletes. And maybe even products for pets."

Elliot pursed his mouth. "Well, you certainly have the enthusiasm for it." He jerked his head back toward Dell, who was bringing up the rear with Eddie Fosser. "What's the story between you two?"

She panicked. "Story? There's no story. We've worked for the same firm for six years. Dell is a senior account exec, and I'm a junior account exec. That's all."

Elliot lifted his hands. "Sorry—I thought I saw…something between you."

Gabrielle manufactured a smile. "Must be the competitive spirit."

Elliot studied her face. "Must be."

The sun was hitting the left side of her face and she could practically feel the freckles popping out. "I need to stop and get some sunscreen," she said, eager to escape the attention of the observant man. "You go ahead, and I'll catch up."

He nodded and walked ahead.

"It must be hell to have pale skin," Lynda Gilbert commented when she walked by. "I don't think I could deal with all those freckles."

Gabrielle's face flamed and she looked around to see if anyone had heard the remark. From their expressions, she realized that Dell and Eddie, who were bringing up the rear, had. She busied herself with applying more sunscreen and let them pass, grateful for the heat and the sun to explain away her red face.

When she resumed walking, a few feet behind Dell and Eddie, she tried not to stare at Dell, but her gaze kept straying to him. She studied the way he moved—effortlessly, every movement economical and well-placed. His shoulders were wide over narrow hips, his legs muscular. He conversed with Eddie with ease, as if they were old friends, occasionally laughing. Misgivings plucked at her—was it truly the best strategy to take on an account that she seemed so ill-suited for? If by some miracle she happened to win the competition and get the account, what if she fell flat on her face?

The article talked about the adrenaline rush of taking a leap—but didn't discuss the ramifications of a public *splat*.

"There you are," Nick said, walking up to link his arm in hers. He flashed an engaging grin.

She managed a shaky smile at his proximity and implied intimacy. "Where did you come from?"

"Had to veer off," he said jovially. "Nature called."

No doubt from all the liquid he'd been imbibing.

"So, my redheaded Gabby, are you Irish?"

"Not really—"

"I played an Irishman once," he said, adopting a brogue. "And I've been known to recite a limerick or two in an Irish pub when I've had a few pints under me belt."

Ahead of them, Dell looked back and shot a disapproving glance in their direction.

She gave him a defiant look. After all, if she got the CEG account, she'd have to work closely with Nick Ocean, so she didn't want to alienate the man.

"I love limericks," she said to Nick.

"Well then—" He cleared his throat, thought a few seconds, then adopted a cocky stance. "There was a young lady named Gabby, who smiled when all others were crabby. Her eyes I admire, her hair that's on fire, and her legs—they ain't too shabby."

AT GABBY'S GALES of laughter, Dell rolled his eyes.

"That was pretty good, Nick," Eddie offered with a chuckle.

Dell frowned and kept his gaze straight ahead. He'd made Gabby laugh like that before, teasing her. His Irish accent was much better than Nick Ocean's. The man was a lush who wanted to get into Gabby's pants.

He tamped down the nagging feeling that the description was too close to home—*he* was not a lush.

They were treated to Nick singing Irish songs for the rest of the hike, and soon everyone was singing—except Dell. He didn't feel like singing and dammit, his chin hurt like hell. Gabby was right when she'd told him it needed to be cleaned—it was throbbing now to match his hand that had been re-injured on the obstacle course.

And now he had to listen as Nick flirted outrageously with Gabby.

God, he just wanted this weekend to be over.

They reached the campsite around five o'clock in the afternoon. It was a roomy clearing in the woods next to a river that, due to the recent rains, was running full and fast. A large blackened firepit with a grill centered the site. Nearby a block building housed bathroom and shower facilities.

"We'll camp here tonight," Karen said. "Tomorrow we'll be spending the day on the river, rafting."

"At least we'll be cooler," Mike Strong said, wiping his thick neck with a handkerchief.

"Meanwhile," the woman continued with a grin, "we're going to have another competition to review your navigation skills." She passed out index cards and pencils. "Using what you learned this morning, along with the CEG handheld GPS, write down as exactly as you can what direction we traveled on our way here."

While she handed out the devices, Dell cursed under his breath. He'd been so distracted along the trail that he'd paid no attention to what direction they were traveling, which was unlike him. He closed his eyes, trying to remember anything about the hike other than keeping tabs on Gabby's whereabouts. He came up blank, then fiddled with the GPS device for a while, finally jotting down his best guess. But he figured no one else was any better off, except maybe Mike, the buyer for the outdoor chain, who seemed like a hardcore outdoorsman. Nick was too drunk, and the rest of them probably hadn't been paying attention. Lynda wouldn't have a clue, and Gabby had admitted to him on the drive up that her sense of direction was impaired.

He glanced at her and she was writing furiously on her card, the tip of her tongue stuck out in concentration. She was still wearing those great bike shorts, and Nick was right about one thing—she had one spectacular set of legs. Topped by a great ass that he'd seen first-hand, and the rest of her...

He swallowed and lowered the GPS device to hide a raging hard-on. The woman was killing him.

"Time's up," Karen said, going around to collect the index cards. She scanned them, the frown on her face telling the story that the group hadn't yet mastered navigation. "We have two correct answers," Karen said. "Mike...and Gabrielle. Congratulations, you've just earned another one hundred points."

Her group applauded for her, and Dell joined in, begrudgingly impressed. How had she pulled that off?

"Very well done," Eddie said, and Dell could tell the man was impressed.

"Eddie and Nick," Karen said, "I'll give you fifty points for getting very close."

Dell bit down on the inside of his cheek. Gabby had two hundred points to his fifty.

What was wrong with this picture?

"One more test before we settle into camp," Karen said, passing out drawstring bags. "These are your tents, CEG's brand new Weather Beater model. The instructions say that you should be able to assemble it in five minutes, but I'll give you ten."

Everyone laughed good-naturedly.

"The first person who finishes will receive one hundred points, and everyone after that, ten points less. As extra incentive, anyone who doesn't get their tent set up within ten minutes will have to make due the rest of the weekend with just a sleeping bag."

A groan went up among the group. Dell smirked. He'd set up dozens of tents—this would be a cinch.

"Find a spot for your tent," Karen said. "And wait for my whistle to begin."

To Dell's chagrin, Nick followed Gabby and planted his tent bag next to hers. Did the man seriously think she'd sleep with him? Gabby had the morals of a small-town girl. Her life consisted of working hard and volunteering at the Fox Theater. She probably shared her bed with her dog. She was a good girl.

The whistle sounded, and Dell realized he hadn't even found a place to raise his tent. He scrambled to a bare spot and dumped the bag's contents on the ground.

"Hi, neighbor," Lynda cooed.

He looked up, and forced a smile to his lips. "Hi."

"This is so high school," the woman moaned. "Good thing that I've been camping a time or two." She grinned. "There's nothing better than having sex under the stars."

"Uh-huh," he agreed, frowning at the pieces in front of him, then back to Gabby, who had already made good progress in pitching hers. The wind picked up and his sheet of assembly instructions took flight. He grabbed for it, but it twirled out of reach. Then he smirked—how hard could this be?

Pretty hard, when he couldn't seem to keep his eyes off Gabby and Nick long enough to figure out what pole went into what hole. It would be like Nick, he fumed, to purposely fail the test in order to try to share Gabby's tent.

And, he conceded miserably, after the way he'd snapped at her earlier, she had every reason to cozy up to the good-looking, smooth-talking celebrity.

"Finished!" Gabby said triumphantly, her smile as big as the Grand Canyon.

Damn, another hundred points for finishing first.

One by one, everyone finished...except Dell. Without the instructions, he had to take things apart and start over...twice.

"Time!" Karen said, and everyone had a hearty laugh at his expense. Dell lifted his hands in frustration, angry with himself that he'd let Gabby mess with his concentration. But he tried to laugh it off, even when everyone ribbed him all during dinner around the campfire.

Everyone but Gabby—she seemed to go out of her way to avoid him.

When everyone retreated to their tents, Dell watched to make sure that Nick went into his own.

"Hey, Dell, I've got plenty of room for you," Lynda whispered.

"I'll be fine," Dell said tersely, wondering how long it would take Nick to knock on Gabby's flap. When he rolled out the sleeping bag and climbed into it, the ground beneath him felt lumpy. After tossing and turning for an hour, he decided to move his sleeping bag. By the light of the campfire, he picked it up and moved it on the other side of Gabby's tent, where the ground was much softer.

His concerns about Nick vanished when he heard the man snoring—the star was out cold.

Dell stared at Gabby's tent, picturing her inside, her limbs sexily askew, her body warm with the night heat. With a groan, he closed his eyes against the images, but couldn't stop thinking about her, about her response to him in the dressing room, how she'd nearly opened herself to him…how good she would feel in his arms.

Was Gabby lying in her tent, thinking the same thoughts?

Another hour later, he tossed back the cover to the sleeping bag. His chin felt sore and his hand ached. Maybe he'd just casually knock on her tent flap and ask for some clean bandages. The more he thought about it, the wiser his idea seemed. He pushed up and crawled toward Gabby's tent.

If she were awake and happened to be feeling a little daring, then all the better.…

9

GABRIELLE relented to the suffocating heat and stripped off her T-shirt, dropping it on the pile with her shorts and bra. She sighed and stared at the top of her tent, hot and restless, listening to the crickets and frogs—and Nick Ocean's snoring—through the air holes. She laughed to herself, wondering what his fans would think of him if they could see this side of him, boozing and flirting and singing bawdy songs, a far cry from the all-American, wholesome image he brought to the CEG campaign.

Her body was fatigued with the unaccustomed activity, but her mind simply wouldn't shut down. She was pleased that she'd passed the navigational test, especially since she'd always been directionally challenged. The GPS device surely helped, but the real key had been remembering where the sun had been hitting her face from the time she'd stopped to put on sunscreen to when they'd arrived at camp.

Those darn freckles of hers had come in handy…for once.

And the tent-pitching challenge—well, she *had* been sleeping in a similar model in her living room for the past three months. The first time she'd set it up, it had taken her over an hour, and had collapsed shortly thereafter. So she'd started over, and reduced the setup time to about thirty minutes. Without a squatty McGee underfoot, this time had been a cinch.

She'd been surprised when Dell had failed the navigation test—the man was such an outdoorsman. But when he'd failed the tent challenge, she'd known for a fact that something was up. And after lying here stewing about it, she'd finally figured it out.

Dell had purposely let her win.

In hindsight, that fall of his on the obstacle course hadn't even been convincing. What she couldn't figure out was *why* he would be throwing the competition up to this point…unless he was trying to butter her up, to—as Tori had so succinctly put it—score. With the majority of points still left, maybe he thought he could make up time later…after he'd gotten what he wanted from her.

She frowned. But that didn't make sense because he'd agreed with her when she'd said what had happened in the dressing room couldn't happen again. And he'd distanced himself from her since….

If Dell had purposely let her win for some devious reason of his own, wouldn't he now be knocking on her tent flap?

A scratching noise reached her ears and for a few seconds, she thought she was hearing things. Then she lifted her head and realized someone—or some-*thing*—was at the front of her tent!

She scrambled up, her mind spinning for a weapon. She had a Swiss Army knife in her backpack—she could corkscrew a person to death, or file them down to size. If it was a bear, she was screwed; he'd eat her *and* the knife.

"Gabby?" the "bear" whispered, and she relaxed only a little.

Dell was proving her theory all too true....

She sighed, retrieved her T-shirt and pulled it over her head. Then she unzipped her tent flap a few inches. "Dell? What do you want?"

"I was wondering...if you have another bandage."

"For your hand?"

"And my chin," he admitted. "I think the cut is infected."

She wavered—he sounded legit. And it wasn't as if she were sleeping. With Tori's warning circling in her head, she unzipped the flap. "Give me a minute to find my flashlight."

She felt around the floor of the tent until her hand closed around the flashlight. She switched it on low, then trained it on her backpack.

"Can I come in?"

She hesitated, then pulled the sleeping bag

around her legs to cover her underwear. "Uh, sure. I wanted to talk to you anyway."

The tent flap rustled and her heart rate increased when he slid inside. She couldn't see his face, only his silhouette.

"I'm still looking," she said, rooting around in her backpack. "Here it is." She removed the first-aid kit and turned toward him, setting the flashlight between them. His hair and clothing were rumpled. He chuckled as he glanced around the interior that was easily big enough for two. "So this is what it looks like inside."

She opened the first-aid kit and removed the antibiotic ointment. "Uh-huh."

"Do you really sleep in a tent in your apartment?"

"I have been, one very similar to this."

"That sounds…cozy."

She shrugged. "It's fun. Lift your chin."

He did as he was told and she tried to zero in on the cut, to ignore his bottomless brown eyes and the rugged features that couldn't be mistaken for those of a pretty boy, like Nick Ocean. She smoothed the ointment over the cut with her fingers, over the sandpapery texture of his beard stubble. Just touching him sent her mind spiraling in carnal directions. He smelled of the minty body wash from the showers, and she imagined Dell standing under the shower head with sudsy water rolling off his fit body. Unbidden, her midsection tightened with desire. And suddenly the tent was fraught with sexual tension.

"It's a little swollen," she whispered.

"Are we still talking about my cut?" he asked, sending an electric charge through the air.

He was tempting, she conceded. A hard body with plenty of charm, and years of fantasies on her part to spur her on. How many times had she lain in the tent in her living room and pretended that Dell was lying with her, closed off from the world?

Too many times to admit.

"Yes, I'm referring to your cut."

He moistened his lips. "Are you wearing anything under that sleeping bag?"

"None of your business." She tore open a Band-Aid and slapped it on his chin.

"Ow."

"Let me see your hand."

He obliged warily. The old bandage was damp and curled at the edges. She removed it to find the blisters had broken open to reveal red, angry skin that had pruned against the moisture. After applying more salve, she re-bandaged it quickly, adding an extra layer for good measure.

"There you go."

He flexed his hand. "Thanks."

"Good night, Dell."

He reached up and brushed her hair behind her ear. "You said you wanted to talk."

She pressed her lips together, trying to recall exactly what it was she'd wanted to talk about.

He leaned forward and captured her mouth in an all-consuming kiss. Her mind went completely blank as longing coiled in her belly. A fantasy unrolled before her: the two of them...in the woods...in a dark tent...alone....

The sound of a loud snore rent the air, reminding her they weren't alone.

She pulled her mouth from his and said breathlessly, "I know what you're up to."

He took the flashlight from her and extinguished the light. Then he licked and kissed his way down the column of her neck. "What...am...I...up... to?"

"Come on, Dell," she said, arching into his kisses in spite of her best intentions. "You tripped on a blade of grass."

"Uh-huh." He gently pushed her back, slid his hand under her T-shirt, and palmed her breast, uttering a groan.

Her breath rushed out. "You failed...the navigation test." God, his hands felt so good on her body, she could barely think.

"Uh-huh."

"And you couldn't...get your tent up."

His laugh was throaty as he cupped her hand over the ridge of his erection. "My tent is definitely up."

She pulled away from him, her breath coming in small gasps. "That's what I mean. You're failing the challenges on purpose, aren't you?"

He stopped and pulled back. "What? Why would I do that?"

"So you can do *this,*" she said pointedly.

He was still for a few seconds, his face barely discernible in the darkness, making her all the more aware of his body lying on top of hers, his knee tucked between hers, touching skin to skin in more places than not.

"I'll stop any time you tell me to," he whispered, then lowered his mouth to hers for a long, languid kiss.

His tongue explored her mouth slowly, stirring every dormant sensation in her body. He broke the kiss and lifted her T-shirt, feasting on her breasts, drawing her nipples into his mouth, sending wonderfully un-bearable pleasure rushing through her body. He slid lower, licking a trail down her stomach. Through her thin cotton panties, he flicked his tongue over the heart of her womanhood. She melted into the ground beneath her and fisted her hands in his shirt to keep from crying out. He rolled her panties lower and buried his head between her thighs. She was unpre-pared for the erotic jolt to her system, causing her to buck. She only knew that she didn't want it to end....

Which was why it had to…

"Dell," she whispered, squirming against him. "Dell…stop."

He lifted his head, then slowly crawled up until his mouth was over hers. "Okay. Good night, Gabby." Then he kissed her hard, with the shocking scent of her on his mouth. He pushed himself up, then slid outside the tent.

She lay there, her body coursing with desire, an orgasm languishing. She slid her hand down to her stomach and into the curls at the juncture of her thighs, still exposed, and now wet from his mouth. With Dell's face in her mind, hovering over her, joining his body with hers, she massaged the firm little nub, bringing herself to climax, biting her fist to keep her cries at bay as her body convulsed.

A few seconds later, she heard Dell's chuckle and realized that she hadn't been quiet enough. She squeezed her eyes shut and her face blazed in embarrassment, but at least she could respect herself in the morning.

Yet as Gabrielle dozed off to sleep, one disturbing thought occurred to her: Dell hadn't denied that he was letting her win.…

10

LET HER WIN—was Gabby serious? Dell swatted at something that landed on his face, then windmilled his hands in frustration—all night he'd been little more than a stoop for anything with wings and a stinger.

He sighed and sat up in the predawn light, giving up on the idea of getting any more shuteye. Between the insects, Ocean's snoring and the encounter with Gabby, he'd gotten no rest at all. If touching and tasting her body hadn't been enough to keep him awake, the sound of her self-induced orgasm afterward had nearly driven him crazy. His body had been coiled so tightly, it had taken every ounce of will-power he had not to do the same, but he refused to jack off in his sleeping bag like some thirteen-year-old.

The campsite was quiet, but people were starting to stir. Karen emerged from her tent and began to prepare breakfast. One by one, the participants that Eddie had gathered for the weekend began to appear, Gabby one of the first. He was shaking out his sleeping bag when she rolled out, her hair and clothing sleep-mussed. She shot him a brief glance, blushed furiously, then headed to the bathhouse.

Dell watched her go, conceding that she was appealing, with a body that wouldn't quit, but what about her had him tied completely in knots? Distracted to the point that it looked like he was throwing the competition?

"Nice, huh?" Nick said, joining him in watching Gabby walk away. "I was hoping to get some of that last night."

Dell's hand fisted, itching to punch the man. Instead he glared and said, "For Gabby to agree to that, she'd have to be as drunk as you were last night, Ocean."

Nick gave a little laugh. "I'm just trying to take the edge off of this ridiculous survival exercise."

"CEG pays you a lot of money to be the image behind their products. I'd think you'd be on your best behavior around Eddie Fosser."

The man expelled a harsh laugh. "As long as I play nice for the camera, CEG is happy. And you'd better learn to like it, too, if you plan to take over this account." Nick grinned. "Although, I have to admit, Gabby is my first choice."

Nick walked away and Dell ground his teeth. Fuming, he rolled his sleeping bag and bound it with straps. He skipped the bathhouse and went to the riverbank to cup the cool water in his hands and splash his face and arms. It was, he conceded, a beautiful place, and something swelled inside him when he was outdoors.

Usually.

But this weekend, he'd been so completely distracted by Gabby and the competition that he'd lost sight of their majestic surroundings. Some days he wished he'd chosen being a mountain ranger or a guide over marketing and sales. It wouldn't pay as much, but it would allow him to do what he loved most.

On the other hand, handling the CEG account would be nice middle ground.

He wiped his face with his red T-shirt that featured a cartoon man bungee-jumping with a cord that was too long. Dell was sure there was some symbolism there somewhere to apply to this weekend, but his mind was too sleep-deprived and foggy to figure it out.

The only thing that was clear in his mind was that it had been a very good thing that Gabby had stopped him last night before he did something they would've both regretted. He allowed himself a smug little smile—at least he'd given her pleasure that he'd bet she'd never experienced before…and he couldn't ever remember pleasuring a woman and then walking away without finding his own release.

That was maturity, wasn't it? Then he frowned. Or something else?

"Breakfast is ready!" Karen bellowed.

He returned to the site and joined the others in scarfing down eggs and bacon and juice. Gabby, appealing in a pair of cargo shorts and pink T-shirt, made tentative, wary eye contact and laughed at Nick Ocean's lame jokes as he entertained the group. Dell made the mistake of glancing at Lynda, who was perfectly made up, and shooting him suggestive looks, plus a flash of her crotch in the skirt she wore. He gave her a flat smile and looked away.

Karen stood and glanced toward a crude boat ramp carved into the bank of the river. "There's our equipment now." A bus carrying yellow rafts pulled into view. "When you're finished, break down your tents and get your backpacks. You'll leave your packs on the bus, so take out any personal items you need. We'll be camping downstream tonight."

Dell smiled—a day on the river sounded fun.

"There will be four to a raft, same teams as yesterday."

His smile evaporated. With Gabby on the other raft, the day suddenly sounded less fun…and endless.

After being outfitted with CEG helmets, paddles, life jackets and sports sandals, Karen and Joe gave everyone a brief overview of how to hold the paddle, how to brace oneself in the raft and what to do if they fell or were thrown out of the raft. Having received certification for all paddling sports, Dell yawned.

"I'll be watching everyone for technique," Karen said. "The most important thing is to be safe and stay in the raft—got it?"

Everyone climbed aboard and shoved off, with Karen in Gabby's raft sitting on the back to run the "rudder" paddle, and Joe with a waterproof camera around his neck at the rudder position in Dell's raft.

The river was running just high enough for an enjoyable ride, with a couple of class-three rapids interspersed throughout. But it was tame stuff for Dell, who had rafted, canoed and kayaked much faster and rougher water. He dipped his paddle and went through the motions, engaging Eddie in conversation while trying to keep an eye on Gabby in the raft ahead.

Nick sat just behind her, and someone needed to tell the guy that he should keep *both* hands on his paddle…and off Gabby.

"Dell?"

"Hmm?" He turned his head to find Eddie and everyone else—Mike, Lynda and Joe—staring at him.

"I asked if you thought Gabrielle could handle the CEG account?"

He took his time answering. "Gabby has been assisting on the account for a while now, and she knows the products."

"But?" Eddie prompted.

He struggled for the right words—he didn't want to badmouth Gabby, but dammit, he *did* want this account. "But…she doesn't have experience on an account the size of CEG, and in my opinion, I don't think she's ready."

"Fair enough," Eddie said with a nod.

"Guess that won't matter if she keeps beating you, Kingston," Mike said with a laugh, and everyone joined in, including Dell.

But apprehension gnawed at this stomach. Even though he'd expressed his true opinion, he didn't feel good about it. He glanced at Gabby in the raft ahead of him, setting his jaw when Nick pulled her back against him after the raft dipped and water doused them.

"Rock on the right!" Joe shouted from his higher position on the back of the raft.

Too late, the raft ricocheted off the boulder just under the surface of the water and Dell, distracted, was knocked over the side of the raft by the sheer force. He plunged underwater and landed hard on a rock, jamming his ankle. Cursing the pain and his lapse in judgment, he surfaced and rode through the rapid, paddle held high and feet first to protect himself from slamming into other rocks. That at least he remembered.

Both rafts waited for him off to the side in a calm, shallow pool of water.

"Are you all right?" Karen called through cupped hands.

He gave her a thumbs-up, but as he reached them, he wasn't sure what hurt the most—his pride or his ankle.

"You're bleeding," Gabby said, pointing to his shin when he reached shallow water.

He waved off her concern in an attempt to reduce his humiliation. God, Eddie Fosser must think he was a complete loser.

"How did you fall out, Dell?" Nick called, his voice smug with laughter.

"Thought it was a good day for a swim," Dell called back.

"And so it is," Karen said, peering up at the sun. "We're about halfway through our trip and we're running ahead of schedule, so why don't we take a swim break?"

SWIMMING. Nerves fluttered in Gabrielle's stomach. She didn't know how to swim, partly because when she was young she'd been teased so mercilessly about her freckles and fair skin, she hadn't dared to expose herself in a bathing suit.

Everyone began shedding equipment and T-shirts and shorts on the bank. Beneath her shorts and T-shirt she wore a green high-necked racing back suit that had been in the pile of CEG clothing that she'd tested and documented. Feeling self-conscious, she undressed, glancing at Dell under her lashes to find him looking in her direction. Was he thinking of last night, of how much of her he'd already seen…and touched…and tasted?

Next to her, Lynda emerged from her little skirt outfit as a bronzed goddess, clad in a white bikini so miniscule, it was almost pointless.

Wishing for a towel or a coverup, Gabrielle waded into the water, sitting down in front of a rock to submerge herself up to her neck, but keeping her feet firmly planted on the ground. Nick, apparently lured by Lynda's teeny bikini, frolicked with the woman out in deeper water.

"Hi."

Gabrielle looked up to see Dell standing in front of her wearing only black swim trunks, his physique backlit by the midday sun. He was breathtaking.

"Hi," she said.

"Can I join you?"

She shrugged even as her pulse kicked up. "Sure."

He sat down near her, clasped his hands behind his head and leaned against the rock at their back.

"How's your leg?" she asked.

"My leg's fine. It's my ankle that hurts."

"Serves you right."

He frowned. "For what?"

"For throwing yourself out of the raft like that."

"I didn't *throw* myself out of the raft."

She scoffed. "You forget, Dell, that I wrote your

bio for the annual report. You have enough creden-
tials in water sports to be a guide yourself."

A muscle worked in his jaw. "Let's drop it, okay?"

Frustrated, she leaned her head back and tried to
let the cool water relax her body, soothe her mind.
But she was all too aware of the man sitting next to
her, emanating sex appeal like a radio frequency.

"Want to go for a swim?" he asked, nodding toward
deeper water where the rest of the group had migrated.

She bit into her lip. "You go ahead."

"What's the matter?"

"Nothing."

"Something's wrong, I can see it on your face."

She sighed. "I don't know how to swim."

His eyes widened, then he lifted his hands. "So
let me teach you."

"Not here, no way." Then she gave a dry laugh.
"Besides, you might drown me to have the CEG
account all to yourself."

"Ah, but isn't that counter to your theory that I'm
throwing this competition in order to sleep with you?"

Her breasts tingled. "I didn't say that…exactly."

He leaned his head back against the rock, a smile
on his face. "I heard you last night, after I left."

She closed her eyes as heat suffused her cheeks.
"I don't know what you're talking about."

"It would've been much more fun if you'd let
me finish."

She gasped and opened her eyes to find him looking at her with those never-ending brown eyes, promising her…daring her. But she'd fallen for that one before.

"Stay away from my tent, Dell."

Karen called for lunch and Gabrielle pushed to her feet to wade out of the water, not caring how much of her milk-pale skin showed, or that her nipples had beaded from the cool water. If she acted nonchalant, Dell wouldn't be able to tell how much his naughty words had turned her on, and that now she only craved him more.

11

GABRIELLE WAS HAPPY when it was time to shove off again—at least she and Dell were in separate rafts. Except this time, his raft was in front of hers, which made it hard to keep her eyes off him.

Dell wasn't the most handsome man in the world—his nose wasn't aristocratically chiseled like Nick Ocean's, and his smiles didn't produce movie-star dimples, but it was the way his expression could go from teasing to serious to sexy in the length of a sentence that fascinated her. And those eyes. She wondered if a woman were able to penetrate Dell's ultracool exterior, what she would find there. That he was as happy-go-lucky and shallow as he let on, or that, as she'd fantasized, he had the potential to bond with a woman for the long haul—

Lynda's scream of laughter sounded from the raft in front. She and Dell were in a splashing contest, and he was completely dousing the woman with a few well-placed dips of his paddle. Joe raised his camera to capture the moment.

Envy rolled through Gabrielle at the brunette's confidence to banter so easily with men like Dell and Nick, to loosen up and have fun…

Instead, she and Dell seemed to be alternately adversarial and horizontal.

But since there was no resolving the situation at the moment, she pushed the thoughts of their encounters from her mind and dug her paddle into the water, determined to eke every ounce of enjoyment out of the day. It was a gorgeous, breezy summer day, and the water sparkled like diamonds.

She'd taken Karen's word for it that a person's level of swimming aptitude wasn't of primary concern if thrown from a raft—the lifejacket, CEG's top-of-the-line model with a back neck float, would pop a person to the top of the water. After that it was important to keep a cool head, to ride through rough water with one's feet in front, and to get to shallow or calm water as quickly as possible.

So in spite of not being able to swim, she had tried to set aside her fears about the water rushing all around her. That, and she had her feet wedged so deeply into the crevice between the side and the bottom of the rubber raft, she wasn't going anywhere.

But her own fears had ignited fury with Dell when he'd fallen out of the raft on purpose. He was no doubt an excellent swimmer, but he could have hit his head on a rock, or been trapped beneath the water. Her breath had caught in her lungs when she'd seen him go underwater, and she hadn't breathed again until he'd surfaced.

Damn him for clowning around, for making her care…more.

She stole another glance at him. With his head thrown back, laughing, Dell was heartbreakingly sexy, his dark hair drenched from horsing around with Lynda, his bare arms and shoulders extending from the life jacket, bronzed and muscled. He joked with others in his raft and seemed to be generally enjoying life. He seemed so comfortable in the outdoors, and she was so…clumsy and pale and allergy-ridden. In truth, they didn't have much in common, except a raging attraction that—at least on his part—would disappear the minute she slept with him.

Not that she planned to sleep with him.

Dismayed at the direction her thoughts were taking, Gabrielle tore her gaze from him and made an effort to start a conversation among the people on her raft. Nick was unusually quiet—probably still hung over, she surmised—but Elliot and Wally and Karen proved to be interesting and entertaining.

"Wally," Gabrielle asked, "could you sell outdoor products for pets?"

He grunted. "Could I? Our pet department is bigger than our children's department in about half our stores nationwide."

She glanced at Elliot and he winked at her, boosting her confidence and reminding her that she did have something to bring to the CEG account…assuming she won it.

She frowned. And thanks to Dell, she was on track to do just that….

She expected him to fling himself overboard again during the course of running a couple of more rapids, but he didn't, and she managed to stay in the raft by grabbing the rope handle by her knee when things got bumpy. She was feeling pleasantly tired when around five in the afternoon, Karen pointed to the bridge that marked the end of their trip and their next campsite, once again blessed with a bathhouse.

She'd managed to stay away from Dell while they were on the water, but on land, it would be a much harder feat. With dread building in her stomach, Gabrielle dutifully helped her team drag their raft to the riverbank and up the dirt road leading to the waiting bus that held their backpacks, tents and sleeping bags.

But before they could change out of their wet clothes, Karen blew her whistle. "Everyone receives one hundred points for rafting," she announced, "except Dell, who receives only fifty for being separated from his raft." She grinned. "If you've lost track, Gabrielle has the most points, and Dell is at the other end of the spectrum."

Everyone laughed and Gabrielle noticed Eddie Fosser clap Dell on the back, then lean in and say something that made the frozen smile drop from Dell's face. When Dell looked in her direction, she glanced away. It was clear that Eddie expected him to win and had probably noticed, as she had, Dell's intentional screwups.

"And we have one more challenge before setting up camp," Karen said, gesturing to the black iron bridge about fifty feet above them. "See the zip line? To earn another one hundred points, all you have to do is ride the cable from the bridge to the water."

Gabrielle leaned her head back to look up at the bridge, her stomach churning. At the top of the cable was a T-bar, which a person grabbed onto, then rode down the cable to the still, clear pool of water at the bottom.

Riding a zip line from her living room to her bedroom was one thing—jumping off a perfectly good bridge and gathering speed before slamming into the water at the bottom was another matter entirely.

She glanced up to find Dell staring at her, and she wondered if her terror showed on her face. If only she had time to dig the "Adrenaline Rush" article from her pack for some last-minute advice.

Karen guided them up a short, steep trail that led to the bridge, and Gabrielle noticed that Dell was favoring his ankle. When they reached the bridge, most of the group gathered at the rail next to the zip line and glanced down excitedly.

But Gabrielle's stomach knotted into a ball—she couldn't even bring herself to walk to the edge. She knelt and adjusted the straps on her sport sandals to detract from her nervousness, giving herself a mental pep talk.

Karen carefully swung herself to the outside of the bridge and demonstrated how to grab onto the T-bar and how to push away from the bridge. "Let gravity pull you down and enjoy the ride. At the bottom, let go when you're about fifteen feet away from the pole—see that yellow flag? But if you don't, a brake on the cable will slow you down and stop you, so you might get jerked around a little, but you won't get hurt."

"How deep is the water?" Dell asked.

"Over eight feet deep and no rocks. You can drop in and your life jacket will pop you back up to the surface." She gave the group a magnanimous smile. "This activity is strictly optional, but if you decide to do it, it's worth another one hundred points."

One hundred points. Gabrielle worked her mouth from side to side. She was well ahead of Dell, so she could forgo this challenge…but what if future activities were even worse? Even though at the moment she couldn't think of anything more scary than a bridge-to-water jump, she had a feeling that Karen could.

"Have a partner check your life jacket to make sure it's secure," Karen directed. "Then line up."

When Gabby turned to look for a partner, Dell was standing next to her.

He held up his arms and gave her a sexy little smile. "You want to check me out?"

She glanced around to see that everyone else had already paired up. Resigned, she stepped toward him and checked the four buckled enclosures, putting her close enough to see the water drops drying on his sun-toasted arms and shoulders.

"Are you okay with this?" he murmured.

Her heart was drumming in her ears, both at his proximity and at the idea of being so high above the ground, but she forced bravado into her voice. "Sure."

She hooked her fingers around the narrow part of the jacket where the front panels met the shoulder panels and tugged upward as Karen had demonstrated to check for looseness. The jacket didn't budge.

"You pass," she said with a smile, then stood still to allow Dell to inspect her life jacket.

She looked over his shoulder while he took his time inspecting the buckles fastened over her chest. Even without looking at him, the man's body was like a force field, breaking down her defenses….

"You have a strap that's twisted," he said, and

proceeded to unhook one buckle and fix the strap, managing to yank her very close to him in the process. She held her breath, fighting the pull of him that grew stronger as the distance between their bodies closed.

He hooked his fingers around her life jacket, his warm fingers skimming the tops of her breasts, sending little jolts of desire spiking through her body. When he tugged upward on the shoulder panels, he practically lifted her off the ground, but at least her jacket didn't budge.

"You're all set," he said, then lifted her chin with his finger, forcing her to look at him. "Gabby, are you sure you want to do this? We can both sit this one out. My ankle is a little sore."

Her lips parted. Dell knew she couldn't swim, probably could tell that she was scared. And he was offering to forgo the challenge if she was afraid to lose points to him. Again, he was throwing the competition…because he didn't think she was up to it?

"No," she said, then inhaled deeply for strength. "I'm fine. It looks like—" *suicide* "—fun."

He dropped his hand and narrowed his eyes. "Are you sure?"

"Yes."

He sighed and looked unconvinced of her ability, which, she realized, made her want to prove him wrong.

There were worse ways to die.

"Is everyone ready?" Karen asked. "Anyone want to sit this one out?"

Gabrielle felt Dell's eyes on her, but twined her fingers to resist the urge to raise her hand.

"Joe will go first so he can get photos of everyone, and I'll bring up the rear," Karen said.

With his waterproof camera around his neck, Joe unhooked the T-bar, grabbed on and athletically pushed away from the bridge, bending his knees and whooping with glee as he descended faster and faster, then dropping to splash into the water like a kid.

Everyone on the bridge applauded wildly, and Karen pulled up the T-bar with the second line attached to it. Eddie took his place next and pushed his big body away from the bridge with a powerful thrust. He zoomed to the bottom at a fantastic speed, dropping at the bottom in a cannonball formation. When he bobbed to the surface, he pumped his fist in the air and gave a rebel yell.

One by one, they descended—Lynda, Nick, Elliot, Mike and Wally—and Gabrielle's nerves became more and more frazzled, knowing her turn was near.

"Ready?" Karen asked her.

She was still hanging back from the edge. "Uh—"

Suddenly Dell's voice was near her ear. "What are you more afraid of—the height or the water?"

Too frightened to lie, she whispered, "The water."

"Don't worry, I'll catch you," he murmured, then stepped up and climbed over the side of the bridge. "See you down there," he called over his shoulder, then grabbed the T-bar and shoved off. She watched him ride down, going faster and faster, then dropping cleanly into the water, surfacing a few seconds later. He grinned and cupped his hands over his mouth, "Come on, Gabby—it's fun!"

She walked to the side and swayed when she looked down and realized how high she was.

"Don't look down!" he yelled. "Don't think about it—just do it!"

"Don't let him beat you," Karen muttered. "Come on, I'll help you out."

Gabrielle accepted her assistance. And even though she didn't look down, she could feel the chasm of open air beneath her, and the sensation made her want to become one with the bridge. She reached up to grab onto the T-bar, but then froze.

She couldn't do it.

Perspiration dripped down her back.

"Come on, Gabby!" Dell yelled, waving his arms.

But she was paralyzed with fear. She couldn't make herself jump. The hundred points wasn't worth it. In fact, she couldn't imagine anything that would make her leave the relative safety of where she stood and hurl herself over the edge.

"Gabby," Dell shouted, "I dare you!"

His words sliced through the sludge of her immobilized brain to stir her defiance and propel her forward. Before she could think about what she was doing, she stepped off into thin air.

12

THE FIRST FEW seconds of being airborne were as close as Gabrielle had ever come to dying. She thought that her heart had stopped beating, but realized instead that it had lodged firmly in her throat. The weightlessness of sliding along the cable made her feel as if she were flying, and the air rushing by reminded her of being on a roller-coaster ride.

She knew her mouth was open, because she vaguely registered the fact that she was screaming at the top of her lungs. Below her, Dell was coming closer and closer, faster and faster—

"Let go, Gabby! Now!"

She did, hoping she would slip gracefully into the water. But self-preservation took over, and she flailed, fighting the idea of going underwater. Her foot connected with something solid, followed by an *oof,* then she fell butt-first into the water.

She went deaf for a few seconds, then the sound of her own heartbeat pulsed in her ears. She opened her eyes, surprised that she could see underwater and how green everything looked—Dell, for instance. He smiled, then clasped her hand, and she realized when the bubbles fizzing from her clothes changed directions that they were floating up. Suddenly her head broke the surface, her ears cleared and she realized that everyone was cheering.

Dell was bobbing next to her, and she welled up with happiness and relief that she'd made it alive. A surge of exhilaration like she'd never known buoyed her entire body. "I did it!"

"Wasn't it fun?" he asked, his dark eyes shining, his grin wide.

She nodded happily, and something...*strange* passed between them...a connection that surpassed the physical banter that had kept them at odds, and shook her to her core. God, there was no going back—she was completely in love with this man. The realization hit her harder than she'd hit the water.

But when she noticed that blood dripped from a cut below his left eyebrow, her eyes widened. "You're hurt."

He reached up to touch the injury and looked rueful. "You kick like a mule."

She gasped. "I did that?"

He winced and nodded. "Upon entry."

Gabrielle covered her mouth. "I'm so sorry."

He shook his head dismissively. "Don't worry about it. It's just a scratch."

His carefree expression tugged on her heart as she remembered his coaching and cajoling. He could have narrowed the gap in the competition by letting her back out, but instead he had done everything in his power to get her to jump and to make her feel safe.

"Dell—"

"Watch out below!"

They looked up to see Karen zipping toward their group and paddled their way toward the bank to make room for her hearty splash. When they waded out, they were caught up in Eddie's conversation about the popularity of zip lines in backyard playgrounds, and the moment was lost.

Karen announced that everyone would receive their one hundred points, and the group dismantled so everyone could take a much-needed hot shower. In the bathhouse, Gabrielle undressed slowly, the day's events on her mind, and stepped under the soothing warm spray with a sigh of relief. Her muscles ached from yesterday's obstacle course, and her arms felt shaky from paddling all day. And her mind felt blindsided from the unexpected revelation that she was head over heels in love with Dell.

Oh, sure, she'd lusted after him for years, had endured his teasing and had been rescued by him more than once from a humiliating situation, had harbored a deep crush for him. But she'd always looked at Dell as she might a celebrity—admiring him from afar, but deep down knowing that any interaction with him was fantasy on her part and mercy-flirting on his part.

She hadn't expected to fall for him so utterly, to the point that her heart was susceptible.

Lamenting her stupidity, she turned off the shower and wrapped a towel around her, then stepped out. When she looked up, Lynda stood in front of a sink, completely nude, smoking a cigarette and applying cream to her face. The woman was toned and brown, with the kind of medium-sized, perky breasts that lent themselves to wearing no bra. She was a very attractive woman, and she knew it.

Gabrielle averted her gaze as she carried her toiletry bag to the sink next to her. Lynda took a drag on her cigarette. "How are you holding up?"

Tightening the closure of her towel, she murmured, "Fine, I guess. You?"

"God, what I wouldn't give to sleep in a bed tonight." She grinned. "Preferably with a horny man."

Gabrielle forced a smile to her mouth and turned her back to dress. She could feel Lynda's eyes on her…judging her. It was like gym class all over again.

"So," Lynda said behind her, "you and Dell."

Fastening her industrial-strength bra, Gabrielle said over her shoulder, "What about me and Dell?"

"Are you two an item?"

"No." She pulled a T-shirt over her head and re-trieved a pair of shorts from her pack.

"Really? Because I detected a certain...*tension* between you two."

A flush burned Gabrielle's neck. She stepped into the shorts, then turned around to face Lynda. "There's nothing between me and Dell except this competition."

"Which you seem to be winning—with his help."

Gabrielle lifted her hands. "You'll have to ask him about that."

"I will. So...just to be clear, it's okay if I...go for it?"

Jealousy streaked through her chest. "I thought you and Nick seemed to be connecting."

"Nick is a fox, but he's no good to me drunk. Dell, on the other hand—" A sly smile curved the brunette's mouth. "We have history."

Gabrielle bit down on the inside of her cheek. "Oh? Well, don't let me stop you from making more." She shoved her feet into her sandals and picked up her pack, moving toward the door.

"Gabrielle."

She turned back, her pulse erratic.

"Eddie wants Dell on this account, and so do I, albeit for different reasons." Lynda leaned against the sink and took another draw on her cigarette. "You're a nice girl, but you seem a little out of your element—here and in this business. It's obvious that Dell is letting you win this competition, perhaps out of some sense of chivalry, but what kind of victory would that be? Maybe you should just concede gracefully."

Gabrielle's chest rose and fell as her mind spun for a reply. If she did get the CEG account, she'd have to work with this woman. On the other hand, it was best if Lynda Gilbert knew right away that she wasn't dealing with a pushover…anymore.

"Why don't you let me worry about my goals this weekend, Lynda? And I'll let you worry about yours."

She turned and walked out of the bathhouse, wondering where she'd gotten the nerve to stand up to the woman.

Although compared to jumping off a fifty-foot bridge, it had been easy.

She almost collided with Dell, who was coming out of the men's side of the bathhouse, limping. He wore another bad T-shirt, this one purple, and looked so handsome she wanted to touch him.

"Hey," he said, coming up short with a little laugh. "I feel better, how about you?"

She nodded, cringing at the sight of his left eye, that was darkly bruised. "Your eye looks terrible—I'm so sorry."

"Don't worry about it. It's just a bruise."

"And your ankle?"

"Just a sprain."

"How's your hand?"

"Healing."

"And your chin?"

He gave a little frown. "If you're trying to remind me how old and beat up I am, it's working."

She smiled and the thought crossed her mind that she should tell him that Lynda had him in her sights. But she decided that Dell could take care of himself, and might not be opposed to the idea of being caught by the beautiful, successful woman. Lynda could certainly make things easier for him if he got the CEG account.

She was quiet and kept to herself during dinner around the campfire and afterward, when Nick broke out a bottle of rum and a bottle of cranberry juice. She declined a drink and pulled Karen aside.

"You're winning," Karen said, smiling wide.

Gabrielle smiled and nodded, then glanced across the way at Dell, his face even more handsome in the light of the campfire as he laughed and talked with the others. She glanced back. "That's what I wanted to talk to you about. I didn't deserve the points for the zip line, and I want you to deduct them from my score."

"But…you did it. You went from top to bottom, that was all that was required."

Gabrielle's cheeks warmed. "Karen, you and I both know I was paralyzed up there. I wouldn't have jumped if…"

Karen nodded toward the campfire. "If Dell hadn't talked you down."

"Right. Which is why it isn't fair that I receive the same number of points that Dell did, considering we're competing. I just wouldn't feel right."

Karen stared at her for a minute, her eyes narrowed. Then she lifted her hands. "All right. I'll deduct fifty points from your score. That gives you four hundred fifty and Dell, let's see—" She scratched her chin. "Two hundred."

"Yes. Thank you."

"You're welcome. I hope you don't regret it." Karen smiled and shook her head, then made her way back to the campfire.

Gabrielle glanced back at Dell's profile, wondering if he would ever know what it had meant to her that he took the time to persuade her to jump.

He laughed at something someone said, and she realized suddenly that Dell probably would have done what he'd done for anyone…for a stranger. She had no business reading anything into it, for thinking that he had feelings for her….

Feeling pensive, she walked a few feet away to check her cell phone for a signal. When her signal bars spiked, she dialed Tori's number. After a couple of rings, her friend's sleep-muffled voice came on the line.

"Hello?"

"Were you asleep?" Gabrielle asked, checking her watch. "I'm sorry, I didn't realize it was so late."

"It's okay," Tori mumbled. "By the way, you neglected to mention that your dog snores."

"Oh…yeah, I forgot. Sorry. How was the show at the Fox?"

"Fine." Tori yawned. "Everyone asked where you were. Mattie knitted us both a cozy for our spare toilet paper roll. I think I'm going to incorporate it into a marketing program."

Gabrielle laughed.

"How's everything in the mountains?"

"I jumped off a bridge today."

"Was it on fire?"

"No, it was part of the competition."

"And who's winning?"

She pressed her lips together. "I'm still ahead of Dell."

"Wow, did he break a leg or something?"

"Funny." Although he *was* pretty banged up.

"And has he…you know?"

"What?"

"Made a move on you?"

Gabrielle sighed. "Tori, drop it."

"Oh, my God—he's getting to you, I can tell from your voice."

"What you hear in my voice is exhaustion."

"Have you gotten me Nick Ocean's autograph yet?"

"No, but I will." But when she glanced toward the campfire, it appeared the man was well on his way to getting sloshed. Others were making their way toward their respective tents. To her relief, Dell was spreading his sleeping bag on the other side of the campsite, away from her tent.

But to her dismay, Lynda leaned down and whispered in his ear.

"Gabrielle, are you there?"

"Uh, yeah." She turned her back on the scene. "What did you say?"

"I said that I met someone while walking McGee in the park."

Gabrielle smiled. "That's great. Was he walking his dog, too?"

"Not exactly."

"What, exactly?"

"He's in advertising."

"Meaning?"

"Meaning…he was dressed up like a big hot dog and giving away little weenies."

Gabrielle put her hand over her mouth to smother a laugh.

"You're laughing, aren't you?"

"No," Gabrielle said, then lost the battle and laughed. "It's…cute."

"I'm going back to sleep now," Tori said irritably.

"Tori, don't be mad." But her friend had already hung up. Gabrielle laughed at the picture her friend's story conjured up, then turned off her phone. When she turned around, she glanced across the campsite to see Dell's sleeping bag, empty. And Lynda was nowhere to be seen. So had he decided to sleep in the woman's tent tonight?

She retreated to her own tent, trying to convince herself that the idea of the two of them together didn't bother her. They had history—she and Dell had…nothing.

She needed to keep her eye on the prize, which was the CEG account. Wasn't that the reason she was putting herself through this weekend? When had her head—and heart—gotten sidetracked?

Inside her tent, she zipped the flap securely, stripped to her underwear and lay down on top of her sleeping bag. But she pulsed with an ache deeper than the muscle soreness that plagued her body. Eyes open or closed, Dell consumed her thoughts. He'd gotten under her skin and inside her heart and—

A scratching noise sounded outside.

Gabrielle lifted her head. And it sounded as if he wanted inside her tent.

13

DELL FELT like a teenager, crouching at the front of Gabby's tent, glancing around the quiet campsite, relieved that Lynda had finally taken the hint that he wasn't interested and had gone to bed alone.

He massaged his aching head above his cut and bruised eye. Maybe he'd gotten a concussion when Gabby had accidentally kicked him—why else would he have turned down a sure thing with Lynda to crawl to Gabby's tent and risk being turned down himself?

Not that he was going to ask her to *do* anything—he'd vowed only to look, not touch. Why it had seemed so important to talk to her at this late hour, he wasn't sure.

He scratched on the tent again. "Gabby? Are you awake?"

He was ready to turn away when the zipper came down a few inches. "Dell? What do you want?"

She'd never let him in if he told her the truth. "Bandages—do you have any more?"

After a few minutes' hesitation, the zipper came

down the rest of the way. He happily took that as an invitation and slid inside. Gabby was digging through her pack by flashlight. He could smell the fruity scent of her shampoo. His cock jumped like one of Pavlov's dogs.

When she turned around, she held a roll of bandages, tape and the tube of salve. "Does your hand need to be redressed?"

"Yeah, if you have enough."

"I have enough," she said in that gentle voice of hers that he couldn't seem to get out of his head.

He offered his hand, relinquishing himself to her tender ministrations. She concentrated on her task while he concentrated on her. Her fiery hair was pulled back into a fat ponytail, exposing her long, slender neck and the little curls along her hairline. She must have hastily pulled on her T-shirt since it was inside-out.

She made a rueful noise in her throat when she pulled away the bandage. The tight, blistered skin had broken open and bled again today with all the paddling. He barely noticed the pain of having the salve applied. Her fingers were long and graceful, and bare of rings.

"Gabby, do you have a boyfriend?"

"No. Just a dog." She smiled. "Although Tori thinks the two experiences are very similar."

"Tori, who doesn't like me?"

"She doesn't know you," she said, ever the diplomat.

"Do *you* like me?" he asked, not sure that anything good would come out of this line of questioning, but perversely interested in her answer.

"I don't know you, either," she murmured, then looked him in the eye. "Except as a tease."

That made him smile. "I don't think I've ever been called a tease before."

"Isn't that what you've always done—tease me? And now you're teasing me with this competition."

He frowned, annoyed that the subject had gotten back around to work. Worse...he was acting so out of character that she thought he was throwing the competition. How could he admit that she had him so preoccupied that he wasn't firing on all cylinders?

She replaced the adhesive bandage on his chin, then leaned in to scrutinize the newest cut on his eye. She looked so pained when she applied salve to it that he bit back the grunt that rose to the back of his throat.

"You should get some ice from the cooler for that eye," she murmured. "I'm so sorry—I feel terrible."

"It was worth it to see you jump."

She carefully bandaged the cut. "I didn't get to thank you."

Her face was mere inches from his and he swallowed to keep from kissing her. Hadn't he promised himself he would look, but not touch? "Thank me for what?"

"You knew I was petrified. You stayed behind to help me. You convinced me to jump, knew just what to say."

He grinned. "You mean the dare? Well, I figured if it worked once…" His voice trailed off, and he thought that the first time he'd dared her had been at his own expense as well.

What about this woman made him do things that were counter to his own interests?

"Anyway, I'm glad I did it," she said. "And I wouldn't have if you hadn't…talked me into it."

She smoothed her fingers over the bandage on his eye and he caught her hand. "Is there anything else I can talk you into?"

Her lips parted and her chest rose—she wasn't immune to him. He brought her hand to his mouth and kissed her palm, sighing against her trembling fingers. "Hmm?"

"I don't think—"

He silenced her with a long, slow kiss, swirling his tongue against hers, moaning into her mouth. His sex throbbed, then stiffened from wanting her. But when he deepened the kiss, she pulled away, her mouth glistening and swollen. Her eyes were heavy-lidded, and her erect nipples were apparent through her T-shirt. "This isn't a good idea."

"Haven't you ever done something that wasn't a good idea?"

"Yes, and all of them involved you."

He laughed softly. "I'm flattered."

She didn't seem to be amused and pulled back. "Dell, let's don't forget why we're here, okay?"

"That knock on the head gave me temporary amnesia."

"Good night, Dell."

"Same time tomorrow?"

"Good night."

Dell sighed, then retreated from the tent, frowning at the sharp whizzing sound of the zipper closing. If there was such a thing as slamming a tent flap, Gabby had just done it.

He limped back to his sleeping bag on a bum ankle, covered in bandages and nursing a raging hard-on for the woman who wanted nothing more than to beat him this weekend.

He didn't need a dictionary to look up the definition for "chump."

DELL TOSSED and turned in his sleeping bag, wishing he had painkillers for his ankle, and wishing he had Gabby to ease the pain elsewhere. More than anything, he was confused by this... *fixation* on her that seemed to have burgeoned out of control this weekend. The lust he understood—

she was a knockout. It was the protective feelings, the urge to help her overcome her fears, the compulsion to make her smile, dammit, that had him completely baffled.

Women had come in and out of his life, most of them enjoyable diversions, although their faces had become a bit of a blur. And he didn't ever recall having this gnawing sense of…attachment.

He lay listening to the crickets and the tree frogs and suddenly a small voice in his head burst through: *You have feelings for this woman.*

"No, I don't," he grumbled aloud, silencing the insects nearby. "And if I do…it's only temporary."

After a dubious pause, the crickets started up again.

He sighed and finally fell into a restless, agitated sleep. Dreams plagued him. His body convulsed. He awoke with a headache, covered in dew and trying to decide if he could be more miserable.

"Morning, handsome."

He looked up to see Lynda standing over him, smoking and wearing a T-shirt dress—and no panties.

"I'm a morning person myself," she said, then nodded to his crotch. "How about you?"

He swallowed and averted his gaze. "Night owl."

She exhaled a stream of smoke. "Too bad."

"Uh, Lynda, I think you forgot something."

One of her dark eyebrows raised. "You mean my underwear?"

"Yeah."

"No…I remember exactly where I left them." She turned and walked away, rear swinging. Dell winced and pulled his hand down his face, forgetting about the cut on his eye until the pain shot through his head. *"Ow!"*

Irritated, he pushed to his feet, cringing when he set his weight on his ankle. He sucked air through his teeth. God, he was a mess. He hoped that Karen had an easy day planned for them.

Bird-watching suddenly sounded appealing.

"What's this?" he heard Lynda ask, gesturing to a stack of colored vinyl bags on a picnic table.

The group members were slowly emerging from their tents. Nick looked like hell, and Wally and Mike both were bleary-eyed. Eddie, too, looked a little gray from all the rum. Elliot looked as if he wanted to be anywhere else. In contrast, Gabby came out of the bathhouse, looking fresh-faced and pretty in denim shorts, and an aqua-colored T-shirt. They all gathered around the picnic table, and Dell picked up a folder. "It's a letter from Karen and Joe."

Eddie frowned. "What does it say?"

Dell looked back down and read aloud, "'Good morning. Surprise—we slipped away during the night, but left you with all that you'll need. Your assignment—find your way back to the shelter by ten a.m. Monday morning.'"

Groans and laughter chorused from the group.

"'For your own safety, you are to pair up into four teams. The first team to arrive will receive five hundred points each, the second, four hundred, and so on. In the bags provided, you'll find a new CEG safety device with an electronic chip so we'll know where you are at all times. If you become lost, tired, injured or for some reason want to forfeit the challenge, press the call button, and we'll come to you. If a team splits up, or if one person on the team decides to stop and the other person continues on, individuals will be scored as they arrive. Good luck and be safe.'"

He looked up to find an array of reactions. Gabby was the only one who seemed raring to go. "How should we pair up?"

He opened his mouth to say they could hike together.

Nick threw his arm around Gabby. "Put me and Red here together."

"And me and Dell," Lynda piped up.

Dell looked at her, then back to Nick and Gabby, frustration welling in his chest. Gabby looked perfectly happy at the prospect of spending possibly the next two days—and nights—with the celebrity.

Or was it, Dell wondered sourly, relief at not to be spending it with *him?*

14

GABRIELLE STOOD waiting restlessly for Nick to shrug into his backpack. Elliot and Mike had left twenty minutes ago, and Eddie and Wally had left soon after. Only Dell and Lynda were getting a later start, and Dell, Gabrielle decided, looked almost as annoyed as she felt.

"Nick," she chided, "we need to get started to get as far as we can before nightfall."

He grinned and patted the hidden flask at his waist. "Ready." Then he gestured to her backpack. "That's an awful big pack for such a little girl."

"I can handle it."

His grin widened. "I'll just bet you can."

She returned a flat smile, then set off walking upriver.

"Uh, aren't you going the wrong way?" he asked.

Gabrielle stopped and glanced toward the sun, trying to orient herself. "I don't think so."

"Don't you remember how the river made a big arc?"

She squinted and pulled out a small map of the area. "It did?"

He nodded.

The river did indeed arc, but not dramatically. Although the map was so small, it was hard to tell. "But if we follow the river, Nick, we won't get lost."

He draped his arm around her, suspiciously wide-eyed and bushy-tailed considering less than an hour ago he'd been down and out with a hangover. "If we follow the river, Gabby, we're going miles out of our way." He pointed northeast. "If we go in this direction, we'll be back by nightfall."

She frowned. "Are you sure?"

He took the map and held it in front of them with both hands, effectively circling her in his arms. "See? We're here, and we're going there." He drew his finger across the map, then up her arm, his eyes sultry and persuasive. "We'll get there much faster if we travel as the crow flies."

She gave a little laugh, then looked up and squinted in the direction he pointed. "It looks a bit…rugged."

"But we'll meet up with one of these trails soon." He tapped the map. "Probably within an hour or so."

She bit into her lip, still hesitant.

He sighed in her ear. "Look, Gabby your goal is to beat Dell Kingston, right?"

She nodded.

"And mine is to sleep in a real bed tonight. Trust me, sweetheart—we want the same thing."

The way he said it made the hair prickle on the back of her neck, but she couldn't argue with him.

"Okay," she agreed, taking the map and folding it, breaking out of his loose embrace. "We'll do it your way."

He grinned, his white teeth practically sparkling against his tanned skin. "Good. Because I'd much rather work with you on the CEG account than Kingston."

Sharp features, bottle-blue eyes, sun-streaked hair and a world-famous smile. The man was impossibly handsome, she conceded. Tori would give her right arm to be in her shoes right now. Almost any woman would.

Yet for all his superstardom and cinematic appeal, she still would rather be spending the day with another man. She stole a glance behind them to see Dell helping Lynda with her pack. The woman was laughing and touching his arm, obviously enjoying herself. She would probably have him right where she wanted him by nightfall.

Not that she could blame Dell, Gabrielle admitted. Hadn't she thrown him out of her tent last night?

At that moment, Dell lifted his head and caught her gaze. His expression was unreadable.

"Ready?" Nick asked.

She tore her gaze away from Dell and nodded. They set off in the new direction, picking their way between trees and across underbrush that seemed to become more and more dense the farther they walked. Nick's boundless energy and run-on chatter reinforced her suspicions that the man might have taken something to boost his mood. He went on and on about himself—the movies he'd made, the places he'd traveled, the women he'd known.

"Sandra Lily was the love of my life," he said wistfully.

"I thought she was great in *Little Women*," Gabrielle murmured.

"She was into S and M."

Gabrielle sputtered. "Really?"

"Yeah. Loved to be spanked."

"I don't think—"

"And then there was Anita Leland. The woman was insatiable. We did it once in a Jag in a car showroom."

Gabrielle's eyebrows went up and she cast around for a way to change the subject. "So, how do you like working for CEG?"

He shrugged. "My agent loves the gig. It pays well, and it's good for my image. But between me and you, the only stars I want to sleep under are five stars."

As in hotel. She laughed gratuitously.

"Speaking of hotels, did you ever see a movie I did called *The Fourteenth Floor?*"

"You played twins, right?"

"Right. Well, my co-star was Rachel Pearl, and it was the first time I'd ever been with a woman who was pierced, you know, down there—"

Gabrielle tuned him out and kept walking, wrinkling her nose. The pollen count must be high again—she'd have to take another allergy pill when they stopped.

"...but that's how it is in Hollywood...a steady stream of gorgeous women..."

Jimmy crack corn and I don't care, Jimmy crack corn and I don't care... She glanced at her watch and realized they'd been walking for over two hours, and still no sign of the trail that Nick insisted they would come across. She was drenched with sweat, and her eyes burned from the sunscreen that had seeped into them.

She wondered briefly what Dell was doing, if his ankle was bothering him, or his eye where she'd inadvertently kicked him when he'd only been trying to catch her. She thought of his patchwork of bandages—the man was resilient.

"What are you smiling about?" Nick asked suggestively.

Gabrielle caught herself. "Uh...how good a drink of water would taste. Want to take a break?"

"Sure. Although how about something a little stronger than water?"

She set down her pack and, after declining his offer of a drink from his flask, removed a bottle of water from the supplies Karen had left for them. "Be careful in this heat, Nick. You don't want to get dehydrated."

"Don't worry," he said cheerfully. "I have tolerance."

As did anyone who was able to withstand Nick for very long, she surmised wryly. She pulled out the map and, using a compass and gazing into the sun that dodged in and out of clouds, she made her best guess about their location. After a few minutes, she sighed. "I think we're way off course. We're too far east."

"Hmm?" Nick had a glazed look in his eyes.

"Nick…are you stoned?"

He laughed. "Nah. Well, a little." He pulled a small pill bottle from his shirt pocket. "I didn't think you were into uppers, Red, or I would've offered."

"Uh, no thanks. But should you be mixing those with alcohol?"

"Hell, no—that's what makes it so fun."

She pursed her mouth. "Okay, well, since you're *high,* how about we go with my plan this time?" She pointed northwest. "We're going that way."

"Okay," he said happily, and took another swig from his flask before replacing it.

Irritated with herself for listening to him in the first

place, she set them on a new course, referring to the
compass every half hour. Why did she always assume
that people knew more about things than she did?

"Hey, slow down," Nick grumbled. "I know
you're trying to win this so-called competition
between you and Kingston, Gabby, but I mean
really, do you think Eddie Fosser is going to give
you the account just because you win a *game?*"

"He said he would."

Nick scoffed. "Lynda told me that Eddie asked
Dell yesterday while we were rafting if he thought
you could handle the CEG account."

Gabrielle's steps slowed. "And what did Dell
tell Eddie?"

"He told him no."

Profound disappointment rolled through her that
Dell would denounce her abilities in front of two
CEG execs and a major buyer. This, she realized,
was the reason that she assumed everyone else knew
more about things than she did—because they, too,
assumed they knew more than she did.

It was a vicious cycle she wasn't sure she could
ever break, and a realization struck her: Even if she
won this "game," would Eddie Fosser and Bruce
Noble truly give her the CEG account…or would
they simply find some way to make her feel as if she
were more involved?

Nick prattled on and on about his exciting life,

and she began to long for quiet, or a least a two-way conversation. When she and Dell talked, she got the feeling that he was interested in knowing something about her, versus talking about himself. Of course, now she realized that that had been simply wishful thinking on her part. But it had been nice while it lasted....

She bit down on her lip and closed her eyes. How stupid was she that despite knowing that Dell had backstabbed her with Eddie Fosser, she missed being with him? And topping her frustration was the knowledge that he was undoubtedly miles ahead of her in their final task. With five hundred points at stake and only two hundred fifty points separating them, he could still easily beat her.

But maybe it was for the best that he win the competition. That would make everyone happy... except her. Or would she be able to snap back into her role as assistant, forgetting that the account had once been within her reach?

Gabrielle opened her eyes and scanned the glorious postcard-perfect landscape stretching endlessly before them, wondering where Dell was and if she had even crossed his mind today.

DELL STOOD ON a boulder, gazing out over the horizon, tamping down panic that Gabby was out there somewhere with that lush Ocean.

He soaked up the quiet while Lynda was off answering nature's call, his head still vibrating from listening to the woman blabber all day. The more she complained about her job and the ass-kissing she had to do around Eddie Fosser—whom Dell very much liked—the more he tuned her out. It left him longing for Gabby's quiet, thoughtful companionship that allowed him to hear himself breathe.

Why had he let her go off with that guy in the first place? He should have objected to the pairings, should have insisted that she go with Mike or Eddie, who had a better sense of the outdoors and the dangers it presented…and who wouldn't flirt with Gabby.

Then he expelled a noisy sigh. Who was he kidding? He wanted Gabby with *him,* but she had looked perfectly happy to be with Ocean, and that was the root of his worries—not that Ocean would make a pass at her, but that Gabby *wanted* him to.

Dell ground his jaw in frustration, and from his backpack, his phone rang. At this altitude, he must be close to a cell tower. He retrieved his phone, hoping it was Gabby, but not even sure that she had his cell phone number. With a jolt he marveled at how quickly Gabby had become so familiar and so…*necessary.* Would things be different between them when they returned to Atlanta, or would he would simply go back to his corner of the world and she return to hers, crossing paths only on the CEG account?

He looked at the phone display to see a New York number—Courtney. He connected the call out of obligation more than wanting to talk with her. "Hello?"

"Hi, handsome, how's scout camp?"

"Fine."

"How bad are you beating what's-her-name?"

Unexpected anger flared in his stomach at her dismissive tone. "Actually, *Gabby* is beating me."

"What?" Courtney laughed. "You're joking."

"No, I'm not."

"Oh, I get it. You're letting her get ahead so you don't look bad for stomping her."

He frowned—why did everyone assume that he was letting her win? Gabby wasn't incompetent.

Although hadn't he and everyone else pretty much blown her off before? He wondered how that affected a person, being constantly overlooked and underestimated.

"No, I'm not letting her win," he said evenly.

"Oh. Well, it sounds like little Gabby is just full of surprises."

"Yes," he agreed, "she is."

Courtney was silent for a few seconds, then gave a little laugh. "I'm sure you'll pull it off in the end, Dell. What kind of fun stuff are you doing in the woods?"

"Right now we're trying to find our way back to civilization. It's the final test."

"Wish I was there. Do you miss me, Dell?"

Her question caught him off guard and while he was trying to think of the right thing to say, he realized he'd waited too long to respond.

"Guess not," she said softly.

"Courtney," he chided. "We didn't have that kind of relationship, and that's what we both wanted."

"I know," she said. "But don't you miss me a little?"

"Sure," he conceded, but experienced a guilty pang because he realized that Courtney had been more of a convenient habit than a…necessity.

His chest tightened painfully at the comparison to Gabby—and the revelation.

"Why do I get the feeling that I've already been replaced?" she asked.

"Let's not do this now, Courtney." He pinched the bridge of his nose, still reeling over the fact that he'd developed feelings for Gabby.

"I know—you have a competition to win."

"I'll call you when I can," he said, then disconnected the call.

He sighed and glanced over the dense landscape again, glad that at least Gabby had a device with a button to push so Karen and Joe could find her if she were in trouble.

His mouth pulled back in a wry frown—if only *he* could push a button and find her.

"Dell!"

He turned at the sound of Lynda's frantic voice,

not sure which direction it had come from. "Lynda," he called, "are you in trouble?"

"Dell! Hurry!"

He turned toward the sound of her voice and ran into the trees, ducking limbs and hurdling over small bushes. He landed hard on his bad ankle several times, but was driven forward by her shouts and picturing her being attacked by a wild animal— a bear? A mountain lion? And his knife was in his old pack—he had nothing in his new pack to fend off a wild animal except a couple of ugly T-shirts. "Lynda? I'm coming!"

"Dell…*Dell!*"

Heart pounding, he crashed into a clearing to find the woman up to her neck, not in trouble, but in a pool of crystal clear water…nude.

Her smile was wide and welcoming. "Come on in, the water's perfect."

Disbelief rolled over him, then anger. "You scared me half to death! I sprained my ankle again trying to get to you and all you wanted was to *skinny-dip?*"

She pouted. "Come on, Dell. Don't be such a stick in the mud. Join me."

He sighed. "I thought I made myself clear last night."

"Good grief, Dell, I'm not going to attack you, I'm just having a little fun and trying to cool down. Aren't you sweltering in this heat?"

He pulled his T-shirt away from his neck and nodded.

"And sweaty?"

He wiped a hand across his forehead and nodded again.

"And gritty?"

He shifted and every place his clothing made contact with his skin felt chafed. He nodded again.

"I'll bet this nice, cool water will feel good on your ankle."

He wavered—that was true.

"Come on in. We'll be back on our way after we've freshened up."

It was tempting, but still he hesitated.

"Okay," she said with a shrug. "I'm going to enjoy it. You can just stand there and sweat."

She leaned back and closed her eyes, her breasts breaking the surface. Dell frowned, working his mouth back and forth. His ankle hurt like hell, and the water did look cool and inviting, the largest body of water they'd seen since veering away from the river they'd rafted down. Plus Lynda wasn't going anywhere soon, so he might as well be cooling off, too.

He shrugged out of his backpack, then sat down to remove his socks and hiking boots. He pulled his shirt over his head, but decided to leave on his swim trunks lest Lynda get the wrong idea. He eased his feet in first. When the cool water surrounded his inflamed ankle, he sighed in relief, then waded in up to his chest, keeping one eye on Lynda. But she seemed content to lounge a few yards away, her head back and her eyes closed.

His muscles began to relax and he let the water wash away some of the stress that had accumulated in his body since the day he and Gabby had squared off in Bruce's office.

God, he wished he could fast forward past this weekend—he was eager to have things already figured out. He reached down to massage his throbbing ankle. This...*thing* between him and Gabby was affecting his concentration, his ambition...even his health.

Suddenly another set of hands joined his underwater...except they weren't massaging his ankle. His eyes flew open to see Lynda next to him in the water, smiling wide. "How's that feel, handsome?"

His body responded involuntarily, but he put his hands over hers. "Cut it out, Lynda."

"Dell, we're two consenting adults, and no one is around for miles." Then she looked over his shoulder. "Oops, strike that."

Dell turned his head and to his dismay, Gabby and Nick stood a few yards away, staring at them, Nick in open approval, and Gabby in open disappointment.

15

GABRIELLE STOOD speechless to see Dell and Lynda in the water together, naked, and obviously in the middle of something. When was she going to stop believing that Dell was anything other than what he seemed?

"Let's go, Nick," she said.

"No way," Nick said, dropping his pack. "This looks fun." He stripped on the run, all the way down to his birthday suit. Gabby averted her gaze and realized that he'd taken more happy pills. He splashed into the water and let out a whoop.

"Come on, Gabby!" Nick called. "Some things are more fun with a crowd."

He and Lynda laughed merrily.

She glanced at Dell, who seemed frozen in place, and for a few seconds, she was tempted to strip down and join them, just to prove that she wasn't the shy little prude that everyone thought she was. Indeed, a little sexual thrill ran through her at the thought of baring herself so publicly.

She took a few steps closer, past Nick's pile of clothing, following the pull of the forbidden, her gaze locked on Dell's. He looked half hopeful, half afraid, and the knowledge that suddenly he didn't know what to expect from her amped up her desire to do something uncharacteristic.

But a few yards away, she stopped herself—giving in to her sexual fantasies alone with Dell was one thing, but taking part in what seemed to be a guaranteed orgy was another matter entirely. Indeed, Lynda and Nick seemed to be eager for her response, no doubt contemplating how her participation would increase their own physical pleasure. But she refused to reduce herself and her feelings, no matter how inexperienced, to such a common level.

"I'll see you back at the shelter," she said, then turned around and marched in the direction that she and Nick had come when they'd heard the raised voices of someone who sounded as if they were in trouble. She hadn't expected to find Dell and Lynda practically in the act.

She was thankful beyond words that she hadn't given in to his advances over the past couple of days, despite the fact that her body had wanted to. What kind of man could bounce so quickly from Courtney to her to Lynda?

"Gabby, wait," Dell called behind her, but she

didn't stop. A few minutes and a few yards later, she heard the sound of uneven heavy steps behind her.

"Gabby, for God's sake," Dell shouted, "have a little mercy on a man with a bum ankle."

She stopped and turned to see him limping toward her, his hair wet, his T-shirt glued to his wet body, his boots untied. She waited until he caught up to her, wondering how her body could still react to him, knowing what she knew.

He looked contrite. "It's not what it looked like back there."

"You don't owe me an explanation, Dell. I don't care what goes on between you and... whoever."

He frowned. "That's just it—nothing was going on. Lynda was skinny-dipping, but I just went in to cool off. I had my swim trunks on—see?"

She glanced down to see that the wet waistband of the swimming trunks stuck above his khaki shorts, and that his shorts were wet from the garment underneath. She shrugged. "Like I said, I don't care."

"Fine," he said evenly. "I just wanted to set the record straight."

"Fine," she said. "Now you can go back to be with your friends."

"I don't want to go back. I say we leave Nick and Lynda to finish the trip, and you and I pair up."

She narrowed her eyes suspiciously. "But if we arrive at the same time, our scores will be a wash."

He lifted his hands. "Then you'll win."

"But…what's in it for you?"

He pointed to his ankle. "First aid, I hope. Do you have an extra bandage?"

Gabrielle bit into her lip, considering him. She wanted to trust him, but why wouldn't he care about the points…unless he didn't care about the competition. Or unless, like Nick had said, Dell knew this was just a game and that even if she won, he didn't believe that Bruce and Eddie would actually award her the CEG account?

Her mind spun, wishing she could trust her instincts. She took in his bruised eye, the one that she'd caused, and his swollen ankle, and did the one thing she knew was right. "Yes, I have a wrap for your ankle."

He smiled and God help her, her heart shifted in her chest. She unfastened her pack and swung it to the ground. While she dug for her first-aid kit, he sat on a log and removed his hiking boot and sock. Skipping the roll of regular white bandage, she opened the package of wide, flesh-colored elastic bandage, then knelt in front of him.

Just the nearness of him made her pulse shoot up, but she told herself that he didn't have to know about it.

"I figured you and Ocean would be way ahead of us," he said. "Lynda isn't the most, er, *speedy* of hikers."

"We got lost and had to double back."

"Let me guess—that was Ocean's fault."

"Yes, but I went along with it, so it's my fault, too. When we heard the shouting, we thought someone was in trouble."

"So did I. I thought Lynda was being eaten by a bear or something."

"And instead she'd fallen into the water, naked?"

He shifted on the log, but apparently opted not to respond.

Smart man.

She used an alcohol-moistened towelette to bath the swollen skin of his ankle. "This looks bad," she murmured. "You must be in a lot of pain."

He didn't respond, which told her that he was probably in more pain than he wanted anyone to know.

She gently but firmly wrapped the bandage around his ankle several times to give him extra support, then gave it a pat and sat back on her heels. "That's the best I can do."

He flexed it and gave her a wink. "Feels better already. Thank you, Gabby."

She resisted, but couldn't stem the pleasure that flooded her chest over helping him. "You're welcome. Do you have any painkillers?"

He shook his head.

She handed him a small bottle of over-the-counter pain relief, along with a bottle of water. "These should take the edge off the pain and help bring down the inflammation."

When he took the items, he closed his fingers over hers. "Someday you're going to make someone a great…" His voice trailed off, and he looked as if a pain somewhere other than his ankle had assaulted him.

Gabrielle raised her eyebrows. "Make someone a great assistant?" She gave him a pointed look, then pushed to her feet. "We'd better get going. I'm heading slightly northwest to meet the Clay Stream Trail below the main falls. From there it should be a fairly easy walk back to the shelter," she said in a tone that brooked no argument. She would not be deterred from her path again. If Dell protested, she was prepared to press on alone.

He didn't protest. Instead he quickly put on his sock and boot, then stood and slung his florescent backpack and rolled sleeping bag over his shoulder. She took the lead and they fell into an even pace, his stunted stride matching hers. As if by mutual consent, they were silent, and Gabrielle conceded that despite her conflicts with Dell, she was glad to have him as a hiking partner. While his presence kept her senses on alert, it was also comforting on a basic level to have him nearby.

And it was that dichotomy that so confounded her.

The heat was relentless, forcing them to stop often for water breaks. She frequently consulted the map and her compass to make sure they were on track. She had a few flutters of misgivings, but decided that when one was in the woods and off-trail and absent landmarks, one was never truly sure about where they were. It was a risk to pick a direction and follow it, perhaps only to discover that it was wrong.

And that was life, wasn't it?

She had yet to discover if this road of risk-taking was going to be the right one for her, or if she would have to double back and regroup.

By late afternoon, Gabrielle's clothes were soaked through with sweat and she knew she was going to miss having the bathhouse tonight. They were topping a ridge when dusk began to fall.

"Look at that sunset," Dell breathed.

Gabrielle turned her head west and was suffused with warmth and appreciation for the thick white clouds, their underbellies tinged pink, red and magenta as the sun began its descent. In the foreground, water streamed off steep cliffs in a series of both dramatic and gentle waterfalls, just a few of the dozens of formations that gave the Amicalola Falls area its name.

It was truly majestic, and she was struck by the fact that a man like Dell would take time to notice something so esoteric, and be moved by it.

"It's breathtaking," she agreed, thinking that she'd never forget the way his skin and hair were alight in the wash of the fading sun, and how sharing this sunset with Dell made her feel as if they were the only two people in the world, the way that a pioneer couple might have felt when they topped this ridge and gazed upon a similar sunset hundreds of years ago.

"I love it out here," he said.

"It shows." She gave him a little smile, and she felt that connection between them again—electric, unexpected, confusing.

"Guess we'd better be looking for a place to camp," he said quietly.

His words put a nervous tingle in her stomach. "Right. I hear water nearby, so let's find it."

He nodded agreement, and they set off in search of the water source they could hear but not yet see.

The splashing sound grew louder and finally revealed itself in the form of a ten-foot waterfall spilling into a small tributary about three feet wide that meandered down the ridge before disappearing. Dell grinned. "Looks like we got our own personal shower. If this looks good to you, I'll gather some firewood."

Gabrielle nodded, setting down her pack. She

removed her tent from its bag first and set it up expertly, her mind clicking ahead to their sleeping arrangements. But then she chided herself. Dell had slept outside in only a sleeping bag for the past two nights—why would tonight be any different?

Putting the matter out of her mind, she located enough rocks to form a circle to enclose their fire, then sorted through the food in the bags that Karen had left for them. When Dell came back with his arms full of wood, she held up their choices. "Peanut butter and jelly sandwiches with carrots and apples, or vegetable soup with crackers and pudding?"

He looked thoughtful, as if he were choosing between two five-course meals. "Can we heat up the soup?"

"Sure—it's in metal cans. We can put them over the fire."

"Why don't I do that while you take a shower?" he suggested.

She glanced toward the waterfall in the fading light, only somewhat relieved by the fact that it was partially obscured by trees.

"I won't look," he said, then held up his hand. "Scout's honor."

She narrowed her eyes. "Were you a Boy Scout?"

"Absolutely." Then he grinned sheepishly. "Although I was sort of...thrown out."

She shook her finger as she gathered her toiletry

bag and a clean change of clothes. "I'm trusting you, Dell." Not that it mattered, she thought on her way to the natural shower. Hadn't he already seen more of her than she'd exposed to her doctor during any one visit?

Still, her gaze drifted in his direction as she undressed and slipped under the cold stream of water. True to his word, his back was turned as he tended to the fire he'd set. But just knowing he was nearby sent her pulse pounding as she put her head back and let the water pour over her face and shoulders. After hiking for hours in the intense heat, it was heavenly to have the trail dirt washed away. She shampooed her hair and soaped her body quickly then let the waterfall rinse her skin clean.

Finally, she stepped out from underneath the water and dried her body with a CEG high-absorbency minitowel. Another glance toward Dell showed that he hadn't moved, causing mixed feelings to niggle at her—if she were any other woman, he probably would have looked. Had he decided that he'd had his fill of her? Or had Lynda taken the edge off his libido?

She pulled on clean clothes, then finger-combed her thick curls and gathered up her dirty clothes before picking her way across the shallow stream and back to the campsite. When she approached the campfire, Dell was dipping his finger into one of the cans of soup sitting on the periphery of the fire.

"Feel better?" he asked, then licked his finger.

She swallowed hard as the memory of his talented tongue hit her full-force. "Yes."

"Good. Soup's on," he said cheerfully, then used a heavy mitt to lift the cans from the fire.

"I'm hungry," she admitted, sitting cross-legged next to him on the sleeping bag he'd unrolled. On a paper tray sat a pile of whole wheat crackers, a hunk of spreadable cheese and two individual-serving-size packages of chocolate pudding. "This looks like a feast."

"I'm hungry, too," he said, taking the first bite of the soup and nodding in approval. "Why does everything seem to taste better when you're camping?"

She laughed. "I don't know, but you're right. I've eaten things on camping trips and thought they were wonderful, things I'd never eat normally."

"Then you've camped a lot?" he asked.

She shook her head. "Not since I was a kid, but I have fond memories."

"Are you close to your folks?" he asked.

Gabrielle thought of her parents—her flamboyant mother and her loud, good-hearted dad. "Yes. We talk and visit as often as we can."

"What do they do?"

She hesitated, taking another taste of her soup before answering. "My mother drives a school bus, and my dad is a car mechanic." They didn't work for the Pentagon, like Dell's parents, but they worked hard and enjoyed their jobs. And while she was fiercely proud of them, she was prepared for Dell to withdraw when he realized that her background was more blue collar than blue blood.

But instead of withdrawing as she'd expected, he chortled, nodding. "So, the truth about the radiator hose comes out—you know your way around cars."

She nodded, smiling. "A little."

"Any brothers and sisters?"

"Two brothers, one sister."

"Wow, that sounds fun."

She remembered from his bio in the annual report that he was an only child. "Yeah, it was fun…and it still is. We're all scattered, but we talk on the phone often and get together for holidays."

"Are your siblings like you?"

She laughed. "No. They're more like…you, actually. Outgoing and sure of themselves, real movers and shakers." It was one of the reasons she wanted the CEG account, wanted to grow her career, because she wanted to prove to herself that she, too, could make things happen.

"Don't sell yourself short," he said suddenly, his eyes serious.

But you did, she wanted to say. *You gave me a no-confidence vote to Eddie Fosser.* Instead she dropped her gaze and bit into a cracker.

Heat lightning lit the sky in the distance, promising a muggy night ahead. The bright flashes of electricity seemed to symbolize the friction between them—quick, hot and elusive.

"I think I'll take my shower before it gets too dark to see what I'm doing," he said, then gathered his trash and stowed it in the bag they'd set aside to carry everything out with them, the cardinal rule of hikers. "Don't peek," he teased.

She refused to dignify his statement with a response. But from beneath her lashes, she watched him make his way across the shallow stream, then begin to undress. There was just enough light left, she realized with dismay, to be able to make him out as he turned his back to her and stepped under the falls.

And considering that his midsection was a pale stripe against his tanned torso and legs, it was like a beacon, drawing her attention. The sight of his firm buttocks and hamstring muscles sent a tremor to her feminine core, igniting a flame of desire. The man was tall and muscular and fit, with the body of an all-around athlete—a runner, a cyclist, a climber, a swimmer.

A lover.

The description came to her unbidden, even as he turned around, the length of his sex clear against the background of body hair. She stared, mesmerized as the flame in her belly was fanned into a torch. She lifted her gaze to find him staring at her boldly, watching her as she watched him.

Panicked at her unabashed scrutiny of him, she dropped her gaze and began to clear her own trash. She quickly situated her pack and other supplies in her tent. Then after crawling on top of her sleeping bag, and stripping to her underwear, Gabrielle squeezed her eyes shut against the illicit images running through her mind.

She heard him return to the campsite and she listened, heart pounding, as he extinguished the fire, whistling tunelessly under his breath. Her body burned with embarrassment and from wanting him. She lay there alternately hoping he would come to her, yet terrified that if he did, she wouldn't be able to turn him away this time. While she agonized over the tug of war between her mind and body, a noise sounded at the front of her tent.

"Gabby?"

Her body lit up like an overloaded circuit and she lifted her head. "Yes?"

"Be sure to zip your tent flap to keep out the animals."

She sighed against the disappointment, then dragged herself up to zip the tent flap securely. It was for the best.

Even if her body felt cheated.

She stared at the top of the tent, unable to sleep,

listening to the sounds of Dell settling into his sleeping bag. Here by the water, the night noises were intense—the symphony of insects and nocturnal animals almost earsplitting. Even through the walls of the tent and over the racket of the night sounds, she heard and felt Dell's body calling to hers. The longing coursing through her limbs made it impossible to sleep.

She was still awake when the first rumble of thunder rolled above them. A few minutes later, the first drops of rain began pelting the tent. Dell, she realized, would be waterlogged with only his sleeping bag to protect him. She pushed herself up and unzipped the tent flap, then stuck her head out into the darkness. Dell's prostrate form was barely discernible in the dim moonlight. "Dell!"

"What?"

"Come into the tent before you get soaked."

After a few seconds hesitation, he asked, "Are you sure?"

Her throat convulsed in irritation—and unease. "Just get in here before I change my mind."

16

DELL DIDN'T WASTE TIME taking Gabby up on her invitation. He wasn't keen on sleeping in a sodden sleeping bag with lightning striking all around. Besides, it was the perfect excuse to be exactly where he wanted to be.

Yet he knew that crawling into Gabby's tent was likely to be just as dangerous, in a different kind of way.

He stood and quickly rolled his sleeping bag, then backed into her tent and stowed it in a corner. "Looks like we're in for a storm," he said unnecessarily.

"I guess we'll see how securely I pitched the tent," she murmured, switching on a flashlight and moving around to make room for him.

She was wearing an overized T-shirt that revealed her long, lean legs. With great effort, he dragged his gaze away. "What side do you want?"

"It doesn't matter to me."

"Me, neither."

She gave a little laugh and pointed. "Okay, I'll sleep there."

"Works for me. I'll take the other side."

"Uh, we'll have to share a pillow."

"I don't need a pillow," he said.

"Okay, but if you do, I can share. I hardly move once I fall asleep."

"Really? Who told you that?"

Even in the low light, he knew she was blushing. "No one…I can tell when I wake up, I guess."

Teasing her was irresistible. "Well, unfortunately, I move around a lot, so if I happen to bump against you during the night, don't be alarmed."

But her eyes narrowed. "No hanky-panky, Dell."

He frowned. "Do people still use that term? And what does that mean, exactly?"

"Don't make me put you out in the rain."

"There's that dog reference again," he said with a sigh. "Okay, I promise I'll behave."

"Okay," she said warily, then moved to her side of the tent and stretched out gingerly. Dell had to stifle a groan.

This was going to be a long night.

Following her lead, he stretched out on the opposite side of the tent, estimating there were a mere six inches between them.

His cock, he noted wryly, could easily span *that* distance.

With a click of the flashlight, the tent was plunged into total darkness, the sides and top buffeted by the rain. He could sense Gabby's body in the darkness, could feel her heat and hear her breath and visualize every line of her body within reaching distance. His sex hardened.

A crack of thunder nearby made her jump—he felt her body convulse, and heard her sharp intake of air.

As if by mutual consent, they inched closer together.

A few minutes later, another crack of thunder, another inch closer.

And again, until suddenly their bodies touched, and her sigh mingled with his groan. He reached out and found her hand and entwined their fingers. He wanted more, and he knew she did, too, could feel her pulse throbbing against his. His erection was hard and heavy, aching for release inside Gabby. But all the reasons not to have sex were still there, and more—he couldn't promise what a woman like Gabby needed.

Monogamy and marriage weren't in his game plan, at least not now…and maybe not ever.

When and if he did settle down, it would undoubtedly be with one of his "obvious" choices because he knew the expectations of those women—they wanted security, spending money and a nice standard of living.

Gabby…he couldn't figure her out. She was a good, moral person who worked hard and kept a low profile, yet he had the feeling that if they were ever to have sex, she would rock his world.

But Gabby was the kind of person who would have high emotional standards for her partner…and he knew he couldn't endure that kind of pressure. It was too intense, too expressive. He liked keeping relationships on a physical level—*that* he could relate to, *that* he understood.

When another crack of thunder sounded, she squeezed his hand and he squeezed back. A warm sensation seeped into his heart and he thought it was strange to have heartburn now when his dinner had been relatively bland.

But of course it was heartburn…what else could it be?

WHEN DELL AWOKE the next morning, he realized that sometime during the night, the rain had stopped.

And sometime during the night, he and Gabby had migrated together, her back to his front, and they were spooning.

His face was pressed into her springy red hair, the scent of her shampoo infiltrating his lungs. His arm had found its way around her, and was imbedded in the soft, plump cushion of her breasts. His erection prodded the firm muscle of her backside through the thin cotton of her panties. She murmured in her sleep and undulated against him, triggering a surge of raw lust that plowed through his body.

He contracted his hips, pressing his aching cock against her, and gently squeezing a glorious breast. Another murmur and another full body press convinced him he would finish before she even awoke if he didn't pull the plug. So with a hardened jaw, he tried to extract himself as gently as possible.

She awoke with a start and a soft, little cry.

"Easy," he whispered into her ear. "Nothing happened…but it might if I don't leave now."

They were both still for a few seconds, touching in so many erotic places. Then he whispered. "I should leave now…right?"

She didn't respond right away, and as he inhaled another headful of her shampoo, he knew the only way he was going to leave was if she told him to. God, he was so hot for her, he couldn't think.

"Yes," she whispered finally, moving away from him. "You should leave, Dell."

He sighed in resignation, then straightened his legs and flexed his sore ankle, wincing when pain shot up his leg. But he managed to withdraw his rigidly aroused body from her soft curves, unzip the tent flap and push himself through it.

The rain had indeed stopped, and it promised to be another wickedly hot, humid day. The waterfall under which they both taken showers was now a torrent, and the small tributary had swollen to nearly twice its size. He knelt next to the rushing water and splashed his face and arms with cold water until he had his body back under control.

This runaway attraction for Gabby was disconcerting, but he told himself it was simply the conquest that kept his body revved and tricked him into believing that he had developed feelings for her. The pursuit of things he didn't have had always been a powerful motivator.

Take the CEG account, for instance.

He dragged his hand down his face, skimming his burned, healing fingers over his cut and bruised eye, the gash on his chin. If his ankle felt better, he would have kicked himself for making that stupid dare that had egged Gabby into this competition to begin with. He stood and grimaced in pain. Now he was the one who'd be lucky to make it back in one piece…and with his self-control intact.

Gabby appeared next to him and crouched next to the water for a quick washup herself, brushing her teeth with the thoroughness of someone who had once worn braces, and pulling her riotous hair into a ponytail with neat, efficient movements. He couldn't take his eyes off her, loved watching her move, loved—

"How's your ankle?" she asked.

"Uh, stiff," he admitted.

"Are you sure you're up to traveling on it all day?"

"Yeah." In truth, it hurt like hell and if he was really honest with himself, he would push the button on the tracking device that Karen had given them and forfeit the competition rather than walking on it all day. But points aside, if he didn't finish the competition, Bruce would be hard-pressed to justify giving him the CEG account over Gabby under any circumstances.

"Okay," she said. "The sooner we get started, the sooner we'll get there."

Her unsaid words hung in the air. *The sooner we can be away from each other.*

So the stress of their intense physical attraction was wearing on her, too.

They packed up the camp quickly, opting to eat their breakfast of granola bars and fruit on the move. Gabby made no mention of the previous night's near-miss, and her silence on the matter only seemed to ingrain the incident deeper into his brain as they resumed their hike.

"So do you think anyone has dropped out?" she asked.

He nodded, not willing to admit that he'd considered it himself. "Probably. I'd say last night's storm might have been the final straw for some."

"Do you like your job, Dell?"

Her question surprised him and he automatically answered, "Sure."

"Have you always known what you wanted out of life?"

He shrugged. "I guess I never thought about it."

"Never thought about what you want out of life?"

"Right." He squirmed. "I'm a pretty basic guy, I guess."

"But you enjoy the finer things."

"Okay," he conceded, hating to admit that somewhere along the line, the finer things—a great condo, Italian suits and a Porsche to drive in addition to his SUV—had become the basics to him.

"So, what makes you happy?" she asked, her voice slow and serious.

With a start, he realized that she wasn't being new-agey—she truly wanted to know. His mind raced for an answer and landed on a cop-out. "I'm just generally a happy guy." But his grin concealed a nagging question—had he ever been truly happy?

Once when he'd been rock climbing in Arizona, he had topped a formation that had nearly kicked his butt, only to look down on a glorious painted sunset and at that moment thought he knew what true happiness was. But in hindsight, that moment hadn't been as satisfying as sharing the sunset last night with Gabby.

He frowned. Did that mean that in order for him to be happy, he needed to be attached to someone?

"Are you close to your parents?"

"I wouldn't say close, exactly. They're very busy with their own lives in D.C. But we try to get together once a year or so." To make small talk and discuss his parents' latest fund-raiser or art acquisition.

"Do you think you'll always live in Atlanta?"

He shrugged again. "I don't know. I like not having ties to Atlanta so I can move when the mood strikes me."

She fell silent, but her line of questioning triggered an unexpected session of soul-searching over the next hour that he told himself was a diversion from his increasingly painful, throbbing ankle. His limp had become more pronounced, and Gabby had to stop often to wait for him. The device to forfeit the competition weighed heavily in his backpack and on his mind. He could end this all now.

But, no, he decided, grinding his teeth—forfeiting now was a lose-lose situation. He'd have no argument for Bruce if he couldn't even finish the competition, and if he dropped out now, everyone would just assume he'd handed the competition to Gabby.

He looked up and realized that Gabby had disappeared. His heart jumped to his chest—while he'd been preoccupied, had she fallen?

Or left him?

"Gabby!" he called.

She reappeared a few yards ahead of him, then walked back toward him, swinging two long, sturdy sticks. "Good news—Clay Stream Trail is just a few yards ahead. We should be back to the shelter before nightfall." She handed him one of the long sticks. "I thought a walking stick would help us both."

He looked into her gentle green eyes and felt his chest expand with gratitude. She didn't need a walking stick, but she knew it would help him. "Thanks," he said simply.

And the stick did help to relieve the full force of his weight from his ankle. Coupled with an extra dose of the painkillers, he was able to keep up with Gabby's determined pace.

But as the day progressed and they moved closer to reaching their destination, a slow drip of panic bled through Dell's system. Once they left this place, he and Gabby most likely would be working closely together on the CEG account, and one of them would not be happy with the arrangement. If they didn't act on their powerful chemistry now, before they knew the outcome of the competition, they might not ever get a chance to explore this…*thing* between them.

Gabby, too, seemed to grow more restless as the landmarks began to look familiar. When they stopped to eat and rehydrate, her eye contact was furtive, although he felt her gaze on him many times when she thought he wasn't aware. Just as dusk was falling, they reached the place where the group had camped the first night.

Gabby turned to him, her mouth smiling, but her eyes wistful. "We're about an hour from the shelter."

"Yeah," he said, then nodded to the campsite. "What do you say we take a break?"

"But we need to keep going if we're going to get there before dark."

Dell wet his lips. "What would you think about us spending the night here instead?"

Her eyes clouded in confusion. "Here? Why?"

He reached forward and clasped her hand, entwining their fingers like last night. "Because I want to spend the night with you, Gabby, and I have to warn you—hanky-panky is *definitely* what I have in mind."

Her mouth opened and the color rose in her cheeks. After a few seconds, she said, "So this would be just…sex."

He nodded. "I'm not looking for a relationship, Gabby, but I want you like I've never wanted anyone…and I know you want me, too."

From the way her eyes widened, he knew he'd hit a vulnerable spot.

"Stay with me and I promise it'll be a night you'll never forget."

Her throat convulsed, and he could tell she was teetering on some sort of personal precipice.

Unable to resist, he leaned in and whispered, "Come on, Gabby…I dare you."

17

COME ON, GABBY…I dare you.

Gabrielle stared at Dell, scarcely able to believe what he was proposing…one night of great sex in the great outdoors before they returned to Atlanta, before they returned to their individual lives and social circles.

She realized that the fact that she didn't immediately say no marked some kind of internal turning point for her…she just wasn't sure if that was good or bad.

He'd been right when he'd said that she wanted him…last night and this morning in her tent had tested every ounce of her willpower. Having her body so intimately tucked against his had made her feel so alive and so desirable. Knowing that Dell found her physically attractive was a heady feeling, but she wasn't going to accept his proposal simply because she was flattered, or because he'd dared her. The only way she would accept was if she believed she could live with the conditions he had set down—no relationship...only sex.

A night she would never forget, he'd promised.

Wasn't he offering to fulfill every fantasy she'd had about him over the past six years? And so what if he wasn't promising her happily-ever-after... neither had the two dolts she'd slept with in the past five years or so, and they'd been lousy lovers.

At least with Dell she could be assured that the sex would be fantastic.

He was still waiting for her response. When she saw the heat shining in his eyes, she knew it reflected the heat in her own eyes.

"You're on," she said, her voice strong and steady.

This time it was his mouth that opened slightly before he flashed a sexy smile. "Okay. Great. That's...great."

She gestured vaguely around them. "What exactly did you have in mind?"

He reached forward and began unfastening the straps on her backpack. "Well, I was thinking first we'd have a moonlight bath."

Desire pooled in her stomach. "That sounds...nice."

"Then the chocolate pudding we didn't open last night..."

"Uh-huh?"

"I'd like to eat it off your body."

"Oh." Her breasts tingled as he eased the backpack off her shoulders. "And then?"

"And then, Gabby," he said, pulling her close, "I'm going to make you forget your name."

"Oh, my," she whispered in his ear. "Are you sure you're up to that with a bum ankle, an injured hand, a black eye and cuts and bruises all over your body?"

"Baby," he murmured, "I could do more from a *hospital* bed than most healthy men."

She shivered in delight and wrapped her arms around his neck. "What will we do if someone comes?"

His laugh was a sexy rumble. "We wait fifteen minutes and try again."

He kissed her hard and thoroughly, and she marveled now that they both had agreed on the general course of things to come, how wildly uninhibited she felt. She bit his tongue and he gasped, then chuckled his throaty approval. "Let go and for tonight, be the woman I know you can be."

Desire curled in her midsection, loosening her limbs. "I'll get the soap."

"I'll get the chocolate pudding."

As Gabrielle dug in her toiletry bag, a giddiness that she'd never known filled her. How exhilarating to know that sex could be playfully erotic, as opposed to an exercise in awkward disappointment. When she straightened, she realized that the sun was quickly disappearing in a cloudless sky, but the moon was already hanging full and low. The early evening creatures had begun their summer song, and the trees lining the river and the campsite resembled giant pom-poms when they shook in the gentle breeze.

Goose bumps raised on Gabrielle's arms at the delicious anticipation of being with Dell. She removed a towel and flashlight from her bag and when she straightened, Dell stood next to her holding up a little carton of chocolate pudding. Her heart beat wildly in her chest as he took her hand and led her to the bank of the river and began to slowly undress her.

He knelt down and loosened the ties of her hiking boots, steadying her when she stepped out of her shoes. Then he rolled down her socks and tossed them onto the boots. The blanket of moss tickled her bare feet, sending jolts of awareness running up her legs.

When he lifted the hem of her T-shirt, she raised her hands overhead to allow him to pull it off. He unbuttoned her shorts with a quick twist of his fingers, but lowered the zipper with excruciating slowness as he locked gazes with her. Then he pushed the shorts down to her ankles and helped her to step out of them. They went onto the pile.

He zeroed in on the front closure of her bra that was of the full-coverage variety. When he released the clasp, her breasts fell heavily, her nipples budding as soon as they were exposed to his gaze. He groaned with pleasure, but moved on to her panties, running his finger around the elastic waistband, sending tremors of excitement skimming over her stomach before shimmying the thin cotton panties to her ankles and adding them to the heap. Then he removed the elastic band in her ponytail to free her wild hair, and stepped back to take her in. She stood before him, proud and aroused, her chest rising and falling with shallow breaths.

"You are a beautiful woman, Gabrielle Flannery."

She smiled, pleased at the approval shining in his eyes, then stepped forward and began to undress him with equal care. Off came his boots and socks. Next she peeled off an ugly T-shirt to reveal his broad shoulders and muscular chest, but he was so much taller that she had to rise on her toes, brushing her breasts against him. He moaned, skimming his hands up and down her arms, seemingly determined not to touch her…yet.

Emboldened, she ran her fingers over the hair on his chest that trailed lower to his waistband, reveling in the springy texture. She unbuttoned his shorts, then lowered the zipper, her pulse shooting higher to feel the ridge of his erection pushing against his fly. She pushed the dusty shorts down his hips and added them to the discarded clothing heap, leaving him wearing only the black swim trunks. Slipping her fingers under the waistband and around, she pushed down the trunks, ridding them of the last garment between them.

She had seen him fully nude when he had taken the waterfall shower, but seeing him nude and fully aroused was an incredible sight…and feeling.

He palmed his hands against hers and they leaned in to each other, touching breast to chest, his erection probing her stomach. He kissed her deeply, and she thought she might melt into the spongy ground beneath her bare feet.

He gathered the towel, soap, flashlight and dessert, then led her into the gently moving river. Apprehension crowded her chest as the black water rose higher and higher on her legs, but she trusted this man. Somehow she knew that he wouldn't let any harm come to her, that he would sacrifice his own well-being for hers—hadn't he proved that much at the bridge jump?

They waded in up to their waists, the rocks smooth and slick beneath her feet, and stopped next to a large, flat rock the size of a piano protruding above the water. He set the items there and switched on the flashlight, standing it up to make a torchère. Then he sank in up to his neck and dunked his head, coming up wearing a grin.

"It really does feel like bath water. Try it, Gabby."

She followed suit, dunking to wet her hair, although panic set in when the black water enveloped her. But Dell's hands were there as a moor and she surfaced quickly, refreshed and laughing. She clung to his shoulders and bobbed in the water, feeling like a mermaid on a magical night. It was a fantastical summer evening, the air thick with the perfume of flowers and moss, the moon dappling the water and providing enough light to love by.

Dell retrieved the soap and worked up lather between his hands, then moved behind her and sank his fingers into her hair to massage her scalp. She leaned her head back and closed her eyes, incredulous that having her hair washed could be so erotic. He moved lower and lathered her shoulders and back, then her arms, all the way down to her fingers. Then he put one hand under her back and urged her to float.

"I won't let you go," he promised. "Just take a deep breath and let the water support you."

With his big, warm hand at her back, she set aside her fears and allowed herself to relax. Whispering words in her ear about how sexy she looked, Dell ran the bar of soap over her breasts and stomach and down to the thatch of hair between her thighs, then released the soap to float in the water around them and used his hand to work up a lather on her skin. Gabrielle moaned and convulsed when his hands touched her most private places and when she could no longer withstand the exquisite torture, she reached for the soap, eager to return the favor.

She sank soapy hands into his short, thick hair and ran her fingernails over his scalp, then lowered her ministrations to massage the sudsy water in circles over the firm muscles of his shoulders and arms. She worked up a thick lather in the hair on his chest, then maneuvered lower, over the flat planes of his stomach and down to his raging erection. When she encircled the shaft with her fingers, he groaned and gritted his teeth. She massaged slowly, enjoying the power of having him literally in the palm of her hand. She moved lower, to his thighs, to fondle the soft covering of his jewels, and to run her fingers along the sensitive ridge just beneath his sac.

He caught her mouth in a tantric kiss, rubbing their soaped bodies together before dunking them both to rinse clean.

Gabrielle came up sputtering, laughing when Dell lifted her out of the water and set her on the rock. He gently toweled her skin dry, then his eyes lit with mischief as he pulled off the foil lid of the chocolate pudding.

She laughed as he painted her nipples with the gooey stuff and swirled a trail down her stomach. Then he opened her knees to drop a dollop on her sensitive folds.

She quivered in anticipation of his mouth on her

body and when he clamped down on one stiff nipple, she cried out. Inch by inch he licked and nibbled away the chocolate, moving down her body. The rock was cold at her back, but she found its ruthless surface an unexpected turn-on…another new sensation.

He hooked an arm under each of her knees, then leaned forward and lapped up the chocolate between her legs. She gasped at the silky warmth of his tongue, then arched into him as he stabbed his tongue inside her. It was as if she'd been suspended in a vat of warm honey—she never wanted the sensation to end. The tingle of an intense orgasm struck deep in her womb, but she was unprepared for how quickly his tongue could bring her climax to the surface. She jammed her fingers into his hair and thrust her hips forward as the nebulous sensations suddenly coalesced into a core of white-hot desire and mushroomed to the surface.

Gabrielle bucked and cried out his name, vocalizing the most intense orgasm of her life that left her short of breath and with no strength in her legs. Her screams, she realized, had shocked the nightlife into silence.

But she forced herself out of her languor because she wanted to know Dell's body the way he knew hers. She pulled him up for a hard kiss that tasted of her essence and rich chocolate. She urged him onto the rock beside her and used her finger to paint the chocolate pudding in strategic places on his toned male body. Then she licked and nipped at his nipples, working her way slowly down his stomach and to the prize that stood stiff and ready for her attention.

Tamping down her fears that she'd never done this before and wasn't sure if she could please him, she decided what she lacked in experience, she would make up for in enthusiasm. She took the velvety knob of his manhood into her mouth, eager to swirl and suck off the sweetness, taking her cues from his moans and utterances. The textures and nuances of his penis fascinated her. She took as much of him into her mouth as she could, rewarded with a few drops of sticky sweetness from his own body. She lapped it up, gratified when he sucked air between his teeth. She made love to him with her mouth, sheathing and unsheathing him with a steady rhythm, then increasing as his groans and movements became more urgent.

"Ah…Gabby…I'm going to…come. Aaah."

He withdrew from her mouth and grabbed his shaking erection, pressing its engorged head against her cleavage. A heartbeat later, he emitted a raw, guttural shout that sounded as if it had been pulled from his throat. He came on her breasts, his body convulsing, veins and muscles bulging like a weightlifter. Female satisfaction suffused her chest to know that she had triggered that kind of reaction from him.

Who knew she had talents past fixing radiator hoses?

When he had recovered, he lifted Gabby from the rock and eased them both back into the water for another cathartic rinse. He positioned himself behind her and murmured in her ear, "That was amazing."

"I thought so, too," she said. "I didn't know…I mean, I've never had such a powerful…"

He laughed, his voice laced with macho pride. "Do you still remember your name?"

A shiver traveled over her shoulders. "Yes."

He stood and tugged her toward the campsite. "Then we're not finished."

18

LEVERAGING HIS BODY over Gabby's in her hastily erected tent, Dell simply couldn't believe the transformation in the woman lying beneath him. Her wild hair fanned out beneath her, her glittering green eyes heavy-lidded, her red mouth swollen, her pink-tipped breasts engorged, her golden-hair-covered womanhood slick and ready for him.

If anyone had told him that little Gabby Flannery would have given him the best blow job of his life, he wouldn't have believed it.

If anyone had told him that she would be the most uninhibited, open lover that he'd ever known, he wouldn't have believed it.

And if anyone had told him that he would be feeling jealous of her future lovers before he'd even made love to her, he wouldn't have believed it.

But here he was, his cock sheathed in a condom and aching to *finally* be inside her, and he was already thinking about the fact that someday she might be— would be—sharing these intimacies with other men.

"Dell," she whispered, pulling his mouth down to hers to bite his lower lip. "Don't make me beg. Do it now."

With a groan, he buried himself into her tight channel in a thrust that made his vital signs stumble and made Gabby clutch at his back.

Instantly, he didn't want to pull out. Just wanted to stay sheathed in her body to the hilt of his cock forever. God, it was like being in a silken vise.

Eventually, he did withdraw, and thrust into her more slowly this time to prolong the mind-blowing sensation. And if he wasn't already stimulated past all reason, there were her bee-stung lips to kiss, her magnificent breasts to lose himself in, and the longest, most fantastic legs he'd ever seen.

He pulled her knees up to his hips to drive even deeper and she wrapped those luscious legs of her around him, welding his body to hers. Thirty seconds into having sex with Gabby, and less than twenty minutes after coming more than he'd thought humanly possible, he could already feel another orgasm stirring in his balls.

Beneath him, Gabby was gasping for breath, thrashing her head back and forth, clasping his buttocks and rocking with him. And, incredibly, she murmured, "Harder, Dell."

A surge of adrenaline like he'd never experienced pulsed through his body as he rose to meet her challenge. She dug her nails into his back and let him know every move, every slight shift that felt good…better…best.

"Oh, that's it…that's perfect…yes, Dell, yes…ah…aaah…." She tensed, then screamed and collapsed in a full-body shudder that grabbed his cock and squeezed it like a velvet glove. He cried out, falling into her, feeling as if he were being turned inside out as his life fluid pumped from his body.

And as he lay recovering, his head on the cushion of Gabby's breasts, listening to her heartbeat slow, he reasoned that he felt so utterly drained, physically and emotionally, because he was worn down from the weekend's competition.

Except, suddenly he was having trouble remembering his own name….

DESPITE HIS extreme physical fatigue, Dell hardly slept. At first he lay awake marveling over the amazing session of sex with Gabby. At length, he conceded that part of his attraction to her was a bit of a teacher-student complex—he'd wanted to be the man who brought Gabby out of her sexual shell.

And she was out, big-time.

But then his mind veered into dangerous territory: the future…getting what he wanted out of life…what really made him happy. It was stuff that gave him heartburn, like before.

So he steered his mind to where it usually landed anyway—on his job. Now that the end was near, the competition and how best to handle it weighed heavily on his mind. And as the hours wore on and predawn light began to filter through the top of the tent, his plight seemed more dire.

If he and Gabby showed up together later this morning, they would both receive the same number of points, and she would win. Fun was fun, but CEG was the premium account he needed to grow his career, and he didn't want to be remembered as someone who had lost to little Gabby Flannery. And if she won, would he then be her assistant on the account?

That kite would never fly.

He glanced over at her sleeping form and something akin to panic descended. He didn't have feelings for Gabby. He couldn't. That would only lead to a…a…*relationship,* which would only lead to eventually hurting Gabby because he wasn't a one-woman man.

Okay, it wasn't something he was proud of, but at least he was honest with himself, and with the women he slept with.

He pulled on his chin, and admitted another truth, dammit—he *wanted* the CEG account. He would do a better job on it than Gabby. And if truth be told, the reason he had performed so lousy on this corny survival test was because he was off his game…because of Gabby. Thanks to his bumbling, she was, according to Karen's letter, two hundred and fifty points ahead. His only chance to beat her now was to arrive three people before Gabby. In fact, by staying with Gabby now when he had the chance to leave and arrive ahead of her, didn't that mean that he was letting her win, the very idea that had so angered her?

Besides, he'd never let a woman get between him and his career goals before. If he did that now, wouldn't it mean that he'd fallen for Gabby?

Dell reached for his pack and, with one rueful glance at her soundly sleeping form, let himself out the tent flap.

19

THE SOUND of a persistent ringing woke Gabrielle. Her cell phone. Feeling mildly annoyed, she reached for her backpack, but the ringing stopped.

Oh, well.

She smiled and stretched as tall and long as the tent would allow. Little-used muscles twinged all over her naked body, but she didn't care—last night had been the most incredible night of her life, and a little soreness was a small price to pay.

Because no matter what Dell had said about not wanting a relationship with her, last night they had connected on more than just a physical level, she could tell. The little touches, the barefaced compatibility, the sheer intensity—people couldn't fake those things.

She suppressed a little squeal only because she didn't want to sound giddy. Closing her eyes in satisfaction, she reached over to rub the area where he'd slept next to her. But when she found it stone-cold, she frowned. How long had Dell been up, and why hadn't he awakened her?

The phone rang again, and she realized it was coming from beneath the corner of the sleeping bag. Hoping nothing was wrong with McGee, she reached for it and flipped it open. "Hello?"

Silence rang over the line for a few seconds, then, "Gabrielle?"

She smothered a yawn. "Yes. Who is this?"

"Courtney Rodgers."

Gabrielle squinted. "Hi, Courtney. Uh, why did you call me?"

"I didn't," the woman said dryly. "I dialed Dell's number."

She yanked back and looked at the phone, realizing that indeed, it wasn't her phone. Dell must have lost his in her tent last night. Her mind raced for an explanation. "My fault," she croaked. "I picked up Dell's phone by mistake."

"Right," Courtney said, her tone patronizing. "Good God, don't tell me you slept with Dell."

Gabrielle straightened, the woman's tone cutting her like a knife. After all the times she'd covered Courtney's ass on the CEG account. She pursed her mouth, weighing her response. "Frankly, Courtney, it's none of your business."

Courtney gave a little laugh. "Look, *Gabby,* I'm just trying to save you from making a big mistake. Don't you realize this weekend is all just a big game for Dell? There are pools at the office on how long it would take him to get into your pants. Don't you get it, Gabby? It's a joke—*you're* a joke."

Blinking back tears at the woman's cruelty, she stabbed at the phone to disconnect the call. Courtney was obviously lashing out. Dell wasn't that kind of man....

With her heart thumping, she reached for her pack and withdrew a T-shirt and a pair of pull-on shorts, then pushed aside the open tent flap and crawled outside. She stood and scanned for Dell in the early morning sunshine.

He was nowhere in sight.

"Dell?" she called through her hands. Perhaps he'd simply gone to relieve himself, or to freshen up in the bathhouse or the river. "Dell?"

When he didn't answer, she began to look around the campsite. His clothes were gone from the heap they'd created last night...and so were his backpack and sleeping bag.

"Dell?" she called again, refusing to believe what was starting to look possible.

She pushed her hands into her hair in an effort to slow her racing mind. After traveling together this far and persuading her to stop here last night for a night of "great sex without a relationship," had Dell sneaked away this morning in an effort to arrive at the shelter ahead of her...*and win?*

She shook her head, still not wanting to believe

it. Then she looked down and saw the imprint of his hiking boots…which were headed out of the campsite and in the direction of the shelter.

DELL SWATTED at the gnats that seemed determined to drive him mad, releasing the branch of a bush he'd been hiding behind and getting smacked in the eye—his *good* eye—for his trouble. He swore under his breath and looked back to the trail a few feet away, trying to tamp down the worry that Gabby hadn't yet arrived. She should be here by now, unless she'd really slept in. He was a stone's throw from the shelter, could see its roof.

He couldn't do it. He couldn't pull a fast one on Gabby, not when he'd dared her to come this weekend in the first place, not when she'd patched him up and waited for him yesterday when his ankle had slowed them down, and found him a walking stick to make the hike easier for him. Not when she was trying so hard to jump through Bruce's hoops to get the CEG account. She'd worked hard and she deserved a chance to prove herself.

But upon reflection of his desertion this morning, he'd decided it would work in his favor. If, after last night, Gabby had been inclined to harbor any hopes of a romantic relationship between them, she certainly wouldn't now. And this way, she would win the competition and feel as if she'd done it fair and square.

He nodded. A good plan all around. And as far as not getting the CEG account, maybe it was time that he considered a new city, a new job, a new start.

Maybe he'd get a dog.

"Dell!" a man's voice called. "I see you made it ahead of us."

Dell turned to see Eddie Fosser and Wally Moon hiking toward him, all smiles. His smile, on the other hand, was frozen on his face. "Hi, fellas. Er, did you have a good time?"

"Other than the storm the night before last," Eddie said, then looked around. "Where's Lynda?"

"I don't know—we decided not to hike together after all."

"Oh." Eddie clapped him on the shoulder. "Well, let's go on to the shelter, shall we, and see who's arrived." He laughed. "I wonder where Gabrielle is?"

Feeling powerless, Dell looked back to the trail and wondered the same thing. Yet he couldn't very well admit he'd been standing here to make sure that Gabby arrived first.

He joined the men and walked toward the shelter, his feet and heart heavy. The one bright spot was that his SUV sat in the parking lot, so Walt the leering mechanic had come through.

The three men arrived to find Karen and Joe, plus Lynda and Nick, who had forfeited, and Mike

and Elliot, who had arrived last night, having a
hearty breakfast. Wally explained that he'd gotten
lost and Eddie had doubled back to find him, so he
insisted that they be scored separately. Everyone
seemed to have trail stories, except Lynda and Nick,
who looked as if they'd been to the spa in their free
time. Nick's pupils were dilated—he looked to Dell
to be under the influence of something.

"Where's Gabby?" Nick asked.

Dell's mind reeled for the best explanation.

"I'm here," she said behind them.

He turned around to see her standing there,
looking young and pink-cheeked in her baggy
T-shirt and shorts, her long, slender legs ending in
hiking boots. His heart thumped raggedly in his
chest to see her safe…and to face her.

"I thought you and Dell were traveling together,"
Lynda said with a frown.

"We decided to go our separate ways," Gabby
said cheerfully, then looked at him. "Right, Dell?"

He wet his lips, feeling like a class-A jerk. "Right."

"Okay, let's tally the scores," Karen said. "For
the last assignment, Mike and Elliot both receive
five hundred points because they arrived first as a
team. Then Dell was next, so he receives four
hundred points, Eddie gets three hundred, Wally,
two hundred and Gabby, one hundred." Karen bent
over her score sheets, biting her lip, then lifted her

head and gave them a bittersweet smile. "Mike Strong wins the competition and will receive an all-expense paid trip for four to the Grand Canyon!"

They all applauded, and when it died down, Karen added, "And if you've been watching the competition between Dell Kingston and Gabrielle Flannery, Dell scored six hundred points to Gabrielle's five hundred fifty. So, it looks as if the CEG account is going to Dell, by a mere *fifty* points."

He noticed Karen giving Gabby a pointed look, but Gabby appeared to ignore her.

There was more applause. Lynda gave him a thumbs-up, and Eddie, of course, seemed happy and relieved. Dell watched while Eddie walked over and congratulated Gabby on "a good try." Through it all, she maintained a sunny smile and demeanor. When she was finally alone, he walked over, feeling oddly nervous.

"Hi," he ventured.

"Hi," she said, her voice neutral, her expression indiscernible.

"Gabby, I want to explain—"

"I found your cell phone," she cut in, and extended it to him.

He hadn't even realized it was missing—he must have left it in her tent.

"Courtney called. I'm sorry, I thought it was my phone and answered by mistake."

He took the phone, confident that Courtney had been less than kind to Gabby.

Like he should talk.

"And congratulations on winning the competition," she added with a smile that didn't quite reach her green eyes. "I'm sure you'll do a great job."

An apology stuck in his throat, but the words wouldn't come.

"If you don't want to give me a ride back to the city," she said carefully, "I'll see if someone else here can, or I can call a friend of a friend."

"No," he said quickly. "I mean, yes, I was still planning for you to ride back with me." He gave a little laugh. "Otherwise, what would I do if the SUV broke down again?"

The corners of her mouth lifted a millimeter. "What time?"

"After breakfast, say an hour?"

She nodded. "Thanks."

"No problem—"

But Gabby had already walked away.

Dell stood there chewing the inside of his cheek, wondering why he had to restrain himself from going after her. From the look in her eyes, there was no chance she would harbor romantic feelings for him...wasn't that what he wanted? That, and the CEG account?

He should be a very happy man.

20

THE DRIVE BACK to Atlanta was the longest three hours of Dell's life. He would've given anything for a breakdown, a bout of carsickness, an allergy attack or even a thunderstorm to break the monotony of listening to Gabby breathe.

It wasn't that she refused to talk to him, or was pouty or angry like someone else in her position would be. She was perfectly cordial, answering questions when he asked them and responding to small talk.

He considered trying to explain what had happened this morning—how, yes, he'd been a jerk, but had changed his mind, only to wind up being forced to carry through on his jerk plan. But in the end, words didn't matter, he decided, because he was a jerk.

He'd never been so glad to see the Atlanta skyline. "Do you want me to drop you at your friend's apartment so you can pick up your dog?"

"No, Tori's at the office. I'll go over this evening to pick up McGee. You can drop me at any Marta station. I'll take the train to my apartment."

"That's crazy," he said. "Where's your building?"

She gave him directions to a shabby eight-story building a couple of blocks off Peachtree Street. It was walking distance from his high-rise condo building, but the differences in their surroundings were like night and day.

He frowned, wondering how the security was in her building, and if it was a safe place for a single woman to live.

"Thanks," she said, opening the door before the SUV had come to a complete halt.

"I'll get your backpack," he said, hopping out.

"No need," she said, opening the hatch. "I got it." She turned around to back into her oversized pack—the one that had saved his ass a time or two.

"Are you going into the office today?" he asked, pathetically trying to extend the goodbye.

"No." The way she said it made him think that she expected ridicule at the office—had Courtney said something cruel? Or maybe that friend of hers had heard the guys joking about a pool to see who could guess when he was going to nail Gabby?

The possibility hit him like a punch to the gut.

"Thanks again," she said breezily.

"See you tomorrow," he said, suddenly realizing how much he was looking forward to it.

But Gabby didn't look back, just kept walking toward the front door of her building, looking as if she were going to topple over with that backpack. She wouldn't, though. Something had happened to Gabby over the weekend—he'd seen her confidence grow, her personality expand. She seemed more…sure-footed.

He climbed back into the SUV and looked over to see something lying in the passenger seat—papers of some kind…no, an article torn out of a magazine. He'd seen her reading it several times this weekend. It must have fallen out of her pocket, he realized, then unfolded "Adrenaline Rush—Change Your Mind, Change Your Life." It was one of those self-help articles, except this one seemed well-researched and presented. His eyes went to a passage that she had highlighted.

> In your mind's eye, picture what it is that you want, then ask yourself, if you go for it, what's the worst thing that could happen?

In the margin, she had written *CEG account.* Dell's heart tugged sideways. The new clothes, the new hair, being assertive…all of it had been a choreographed program to help her get something that she really wanted, something she hadn't known how to get on her own. She'd taken a risk, and had gotten smacked back down.

By him.

He looked up and watched Gabby, loaded down herself, help what looked to be a neighbor woman with a bag of groceries, and hold the door open for the elderly woman to boot.

Gabby's question while they'd been hiking echoed in his mind: *So, what makes you happy?*

At the moment, Dell realized, not himself.

21

TORI OPENED THE DOOR, holding McGee in her arms. "So, you're back."

Gabrielle reached for McGee and nodded behind huge sunglasses. Despite her best intentions, she'd spent the better part of the afternoon, since Dell had dropped her off, crying. With any luck, Tori wouldn't notice.

"What's with the sunglasses?"

She gave a dismissive wave and snuggled her dog. "I got used to wearing them over the weekend, I suppose."

Tori leaned in. "Your nose is red—have you been crying?" Her friend reached forward and plucked the sunglasses off her face. "You've been crying."

Gabrielle sighed. "It's nothing—hormones, maybe."

"Everybody knows you lost the competition. It's no big deal. You knew the account would probably go to Dell anyway."

"Right. I guess I just got my hopes up."

"I told you—they don't let people like us move in those circles, Gabrielle. Chalk it up as a couple of days of paid vacation and come on back to the anal itch medicated pads side of the department."

"Right."

Tori jerked her thumb toward the inside. "I have a yoga class, but can you stay for fifteen minutes?"

"No, thanks. I just came to get McGee and to give you something." She reached around and tugged a padded envelope from her shoulder bag.

Tori beamed. "My Nick Ocean autograph?"

"Sort of."

Tori ripped open the padded envelope and squinted at the item in the plastic bag. "A pair of underwear?"

"They're his."

Tori's eyes bulged. "*These* are Nick Ocean's underwear?"

"Yeah. They have his initials inside."

"*How* did you get the man's underwear?"

"I'm not telling," she said over her shoulder as she walked away. It was more fun to let Tori's imagination run wild than to admit she'd stolen them when Nick and Lynda had gone skinny-dipping.

"See you at work tomorrow," Tori yelled. "Back to reality!"

Gabrielle threw up a wave, but didn't look back because she didn't want Tori to know she was crying again.

Reality.

The reality was that she truly was a dweeb. Who had read a magazine article and thought she could turn her life around. Worse, she had dared to entertain a crush on a man who was totally out of her league. And when he had paid her the smallest amount of attention, she'd attributed saintly qualities to him. And had allowed herself to fall in love with him. Then was stupid enough to sleep with him, only to discover that he had used her weakness for him to betray her.

I dare you, he'd said of the competition. And she'd done it because she'd believed him.

I dare you, he'd said of the jump from the bridge. And she'd done it because she'd trusted him.

I dare you, he'd said of spending the night with him. And she'd done it because she loved him.

She gulped air and sniffed mightily to try to compose herself. She had to get her act together before she went in to see Bruce Noble in the morning.

DRESSED IN A revamped navy suit and armed with as much ammunition from the "Adrenaline Rush" article as she could remember—she'd lost it somewhere—Gabrielle arrived at the firm early the next morning and made her way to Bruce's office.

In the folder beneath her arm was a letter of resignation printed on the best paper she could afford.

If she'd learned anything over the past several days, it was that she had allowed herself to be pigeon-holed at Noble Marketing—both as a person and as an employee—and if she were ever going to be appreciated, she needed to make a fresh start.

Through the narrow vertical window next to his door, she saw her boss sitting at his desk, his fingers steepled as if he were contemplating some rather important business maneuver. After taking a deep breath, she rapped on his office door.

He looked up and saw her. "Come in," he called.

She opened the door. "Good morning, Bruce. I was wondering if I could have a minute of your time."

"Of course, Gabrielle. Please, come in and sit." He swept an arm toward a guest chair.

"No, thank you. I just came by to give you—"

"Dell and I were just discussing your future at this firm."

"Dell?" She turned around to see Dell sitting in a chair. He gave her a tight little smile. She snapped her gaze back to Bruce, faltering for a moment at the knowledge that Dell would attempt to discredit her even more with her boss. Was the man going to fire her before she could resign?"

"Please, Gabrielle, do sit," Bruce said.

She sat, trying to calm herself, but her nerves were frayed and she was terrified that her emotions were too close to the surface to remain professional.

She could feel Dell's cool gaze on her, and she wondered how big a fool he thought she was. Easy. Needy. Predictable.

"Like I said," Bruce continued, "Dell and I were just discussing your future here at Noble. I'm happy to tell you that you've just been formally assigned the CEG account."

Shock and confusion rolled over her as she turned to look at Dell, then back to her boss. "But I don't understand—I lost the competition to Dell."

"And Dell has given you a glowing letter of recommendation on the way you conducted yourself this weekend—your knowledge of CEG products, your leadership skills, your willingness to try new things."

A flush burned its way up her neck—she'd tried new things, all right. But she made herself look at Dell. "Thank you."

He simply inclined his head.

"Will you be involved with CEG at all?" she asked, wanting to know how much she'd have to interact with Dell, and in what capacity, before she tossed her letter of resignation.

"Actually," Dell said quietly. "I've decided to leave the firm."

She inhaled sharply. "Leave?"

"I just accepted his letter of resignation," Bruce concurred.

"Leaving to do what?" she asked Dell, then caught herself. "I'm sorry—that's none of my business."

"No, it's fine," he said. "But I don't have any plans at the moment. Someone once asked me what made me happy, and I'm going to take some time to give it some thought."

She swallowed and looked away, surprised that anything she'd said to Dell had stuck with him.

"Congratulations, Gabrielle," Bruce said, standing to extend his hand.

"Thank you." She stood and shook his hand, still reeling over how quickly things had changed.

"Oh—when you came in, what was it you wanted to give to me?"

She stared at the unopened folder. "Never mind. It's nothing after all. Thank you, Bruce for the vote of confidence."

"You're welcome, Gabrielle, but you were given the account based on your competencies. The credit is yours."

She nodded and turned to leave.

"I think we're finished here, too," Dell said to Bruce. "I'll drop by later to wrap up some outstanding items."

Bruce waved them both out of his office. At the end of the hallway, Gabrielle looked up at Dell, dismayed that he could still make her connections short-circuit. "I don't know what to say. Thank you."

"Like Bruce said, the credit is yours."

"I'm sorry to see you go," she said carefully.

He gave her a little smile. "Somehow I doubt that." Then he reached into his inside jacket pocket and withdrew a medium-sized manila envelope. "And this doesn't begin to make up for the way I've treated you, Gabrielle, but please accept this gift as a small token of apology for…everything." He gave her the envelope, then stalked away toward the elevator.

Stunned, she looked down at the envelope and slid her finger beneath the flap to tear it open. Burning with curiosity, she peered into the envelope to see a picture. With her heart clicking overtime, she pulled it out, then smiled through her fingers.

It was a 5-by-7 color photograph of her as she had just jumped from the bridge. And the look on her face was pure elation and abandon. She had taken a risk, and the result had been joyous.

Gabrielle looked up, her heart full over his apology, and his gesture, but Dell was long gone. She blinked back moisture, aching for what she couldn't have, wishing that Dell was willing to take an emotional risk, on them.

22

"Do you have the entertainment section?" Gabrielle asked McGee.

He woofed an affirmative, then picked it up and carried it to the couch, where she sat reading the Saturday paper.

She squinted at him. "Do you know that you're frighteningly smart?"

He woofed again.

She unrolled the paper and gasped. *Actor Nick Ocean,* the headline read, *photographed snorting cocaine at party.* She shook her head, knowing that CEG might take a hit from its spokesman's criminal antics. Only one week on the account, and she had her work cut out for her, but she'd never been more fulfilled—and happy—with her career. She was up to the challenge. "Well, it was only a matter of time, so I'm glad it was sooner, rather than later."

McGee woofed.

"I'll bet Tori's underwear just went up in value."

The doorbell rang, and she pushed herself up

from the couch. "And I'll bet that's her and her hot-dog man." The guy was a little eccentric, but nice. She was happy for Tori, and seeing them together made her think that there truly was someone for everyone in the world, and someday she'd find her someone, too.

Later, when her heart had fully recovered.

Steeling herself against the comical getup Tori's guy wore—even off-duty—Gabrielle swung open the door.

Incredibly, Dell stood there, dressed in jeans and a dress shirt. His expression and body language were cautious. "Hi, Gabrielle."

Her heart went haywire. "What…what are you doing here?"

"I wanted to tell you about my new job."

"Oh?" She checked her emotions. This was nothing but a mercy house call from a man who thought—who knew—he had treated her badly. "What is it?"

"I'm the new spokesman for CEG."

Her eyes flew wide. "You're kidding?"

"No. Nick Ocean was just sacked. By the way, I heard that Lynda Gilbert is out, too, for being under the influence on the job."

"I was just reading about Nick," she said. "So, his loss is your gain."

"And I have you to thank."

"Me?"

"Right. I never told you, but the reason I was such a bumbling idiot on the first half of the survival weekend was because I couldn't keep my eyes off you long enough to concentrate on what I was supposed to be doing."

She pressed her lips together, trying to ignore his compliment—it was simply a guilty conscience on his part. "And what does that have to do with you getting the spokesperson's job?"

"Apparently, Joe took a lot of shots of me goofing up and goofing around, and when this mess with Ocean happened, he sent the photos around to the right people."

"Sounds like a great opportunity for you."

"I'll be able to teach and do some guiding, and have input on new equipment development." He smiled, and his eyes warmed. "I'll be able to do the things that make me happy."

She nodded, pleased for him, but scared for her—it would be hard to get over Dell if their paths were constantly crossing at CEG. "So...will you be staying in Atlanta?"

"Yeah, I can live anywhere I want."

"And you want to live in Atlanta?"

"Yeah...because you're here, Gabrielle."

She blinked. "Me?"

He nodded. "You've made me do a lot of soul-searching lately, thinking about where my life is headed, how I want to spend my time and who I want to spend it with…and I'd like to spend it with you, if you'll let me after the abominable way I behaved."

She squinted. "Pardon me?"

"What I'm trying to say is that I'm in love with you, Gabrielle."

The breath stalled in her lungs, which probably explained why her brain wasn't processing audio signals correctly. "I'm sorry—would you repeat that?"

"I said I'm in love with you. I'm so sorry for what I did at the end of the competition. I think I realized that I had feelings for you and it…scared me. I wanted to push you away."

His words made her head spin, but she also had to consider the source. Her eyes filled with unbidden tears. "Is this another setup, Dell, because I don't have the energy—"

"Do you love me?"

"I…I…" She frowned and wiped at her eyes. "You can't just ask a person something like that—what if I say no?"

"Say yes," he urged, his dark eyes hopeful.

She crossed her arms, and her tears spilled over onto her cheeks. "But what if yes is too…scary?"

"Say it anyway," he said, pulling her close and palming their hands. Her heart bunched up, poised to jump.

"Say yes," he whispered. "I dare you."

She took a long look at Dell, saw the way his heart had changed, and that she was in it, and realized that what he was asking of her required more courage than jumping out of an airplane. A surge of adrenaline rushed through her body. *Geronimo!*

"Yes," she murmured.

He whooped and picked her up to spin her around, grinning. Then he sobered and lowered his mouth to hers in a hungry kiss that went on and on. And on. Her heart expanded to fill her chest. She scarcely believed that all the fantasies, all the dreams she'd had were coming true, set into motion by a mere magazine article.

As the kiss deepened, her tingling body melded to his, anticipating a climactic reunion. Finally, she pulled back. "Do you want to come in?"

He looked past her into her living room and his eyes lit up. "Will you show me the inside of your tent?"

"Just dare me." She grinned, pulled him inside and closed the door.

* * * * *

A special treat for you from Harlequin Blaze!

Turn the page for a sneak preview of
DECADENT
by
New York Times *bestselling author*
Suzanne Forster

Available November 2006,
wherever series books are sold.

Harlequin Blaze—Your ultimate destination
for red-hot reads.
With six titles every month, you'll never guess
what you'll discover under the covers...

Run, Ally! Don't be fooled by him. He's evil. Don't let him touch you!

But as the forbidding figure came through the mists toward her, Ally knew she couldn't run. His features burned with dark malevolence, and his physical domination of everything around him seemed to hold her like a net.

She'd heard the tales. She knew all about the Wolverton legend and the ghost that haunted The Willows, an elegant old mansion lost by Micha Wolverton nearly a hundred years ago. According to folklore, the estate was stolen from the Wolvertons, and Micha was killed, trying to reclaim it. His dying vow was to be reunited with the spirit of his beloved wife, who'd taken her life for reasons no one would speak of, except in whispers. But Ally had never put much stock in the fantasy. She didn't believe in ghosts.

Until now—

She still didn't understand what was happening. The figure had materialized out of the mist that lay thick on the damp cemetery soil. A cool breeze and silvery moonlight had played against the ancient stone of the crypts surrounding her, until they joined the mist, causing his body to thicken and solidify right before her eyes. That was when she realized she'd seen this man before. Or thought she had, at least.

His face was familiar…so familiar, yet she couldn't put it together. Not with him looming so near. She stepped back as he approached.

"Don't be afraid," he said. His voice wasn't what she expected. It didn't sound as if it were coming from beyond the grave. It was deep and sensual. Commanding.

"Who are you?" she managed.

"You should know. You summoned me."

"No, I didn't." She had no idea what he was talking about. Two minutes ago, she'd been crouching behind a moss-covered crypt, spying on the mansion that had once been The Willows, but was now Club Casablanca. And then this—

If he was Micah, he might be angry that she was trespassing on his property. "I'll go," she said. "I won't come back. I promise."

"You're not going anywhere."

Words snagged in her throat. "Wh-why not? What do you want?"

"If I wanted something, Ally, I'd take it. This is about need."

His words resonated as he moved within inches of her. She tried to back away, but her feet were useless. "And you need something from me?"

"Good guess." His tone burned with irony. "I need lips, soft and surrendered, a body limp with desire."

"My lips, my bod—?"

"Only yours."

"Why? Why me?" This couldn't be Micha. He didn't want any woman but Rose. He'd died trying to get back to her.

"Because you want that, too," he said.

Wanted what? A ghost of her own? She'd always found the legend impossibly romantic, but how could he have known that? How could he know anything about her? Besides, she'd sworn off inappropriate men, and what could be more inappropriate than a ghost? She shook her head again, still not willing to admit the truth. But her heart wouldn't play along. It clattered inside her chest. The mere thought of his kiss, his touch, terrified her. This wildness, it was fear, wasn't it?

When his fingertips touched her cheek, she flinched, expecting his flesh to be cold, lifeless. It was anything but that. His skin was smooth and hot, gentle, yet demanding. And while his dark brown eyes were filled with mystery and wonder, there was a sensitivity about them that threatened to disarm her if she looked too deeply.

"These lips are mine," he said, as if stating a universal fact that she was helpless to avoid. In truth, it was just that. She couldn't stop him.

And she didn't want to.

* * * * *

Find out how the story unfolds in…
DECADENT
by
New York Times *bestselling author*
Suzanne Forster.
On sale November 2006.

Harlequin Blaze—Your ultimate destination
for red-hot reads.
With six titles every month, you'll never guess
what you'll discover under the covers…

nocturne™

USA TODAY bestselling author

MAUREEN CHILD

ETERNALLY

He was a guardian. An immortal fighter of evil,
out to destroy a demon, and she was his next
target. He knew joining with her would make
him strong enough to defeat any demon.
But the cost might be losing the woman
who was his true salvation.

On sale November, wherever books are sold.

nocturne™

Save $1.⁰⁰ off

your purchase of any
Silhouette® Nocturne™ novel.

Receive $1.00 off

any Silhouette® Nocturne™ novel.

**Available wherever books are sold, including most
bookstores, supermarkets, drugstores and discount stores.**

Coupon expires December 1, 2006. Redeemable at participating
retail outlets in the U.S. only. Limit one coupon per customer.

RETAILER: Harlequin Enterprises Ltd. will pay the face value of this coupon plus
8¢ if submitted by the customer for this specified product only. Any other use
constitutes fraud. Coupon is nonassignable. Void if taxed, prohibited or restricted by
law. Void if copied. Consumer must pay for any government taxes. Mail to Harlequin
Enterprises Ltd., P.O. Box 880478, El Paso, TX 88588-0478, U.S.A. Cash value 1/100
cents. Limit one coupon per customer. Valid in the U.S. only.

5 65373 00076 2   (8100) 0 11265

SNCOUPUS

nocturne™

Save $1·⁰⁰ off

your purchase of any
Silhouette® Nocturne™ novel.

Receive $1.00 off

any Silhouette® Nocturne™ novel.

**Available wherever books are sold, including most
bookstores, supermarkets, drugstores and discount stores.**

Coupon expires December 1, 2006. Redeemable at participating
retail outlets in Canada only. Limit one coupon per customer.

RETAILER: Harlequin Enterprises Limited will pay the face value of this coupon
plus 10.25 cents if submitted by the customer for this specified product only. Any
other use constitutes fraud. Coupon is nonassignable. Void if taxed, prohibited or
restricted by law. Consumer must pay any government taxes. Mail to Harlequin
Enterprises Ltd., P.O. Box 3000, Saint John, New Brunswick E2L 4L3, Canada. Limit
one coupon per customer. Valid in Canada only.

52607136

SNCOUPCDN

REQUEST YOUR FREE BOOKS!

2 FREE NOVELS PLUS 2 FREE GIFTS!

HARLEQUIN®

Blaze

Red-hot reads!

HB06

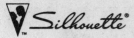

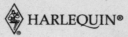

HARLEQUIN®

Blaze™

COMING NEXT MONTH

#285 THE MIGHTY QUINNS: IAN Kate Hoffmann
The Mighty Quinns, Bk. 2
Police chief Ian Quinn should be used to the unexpected. But when free-spirited Marisol Arantes arrives in town, scandalizing the neighborhood with her blatant artwork, he doesn't know what to do with her—that is, until she shows him the joy of body paints....

#286 TELL ME YOUR SECRETS... Cara Summers
It Was a Dark and Sexy Night..., Bk. 3
Writer Brooke Ashby has been living vicariously through her characters...until the day she learns she was adopted, and that her identical twin sister has mysteriously disappeared. What else can she do but uncover what happened by taking her sister's place—and falling for her fiancé...?

#287 INFATUATION Alison Kent
For a Good Time, Call..., Bk. 3
Three dates! That's all Milla Page needed to write a sexy, juicy story on San Francisco's hot spots for her online column. But was calling her ex—bad boy Rennie Bergin— to go with her at her best idea? Especially since she was still hot for him six years later...

#288 DECADENT Suzanne Forster
Club Casablanca—an exclusive gentlemen's club where *anything* is possible, as Ally Danner knows all too well. Still, she has to get in, to rescue her sister from the club's obsessive owner. But when she catches sexy FBI agent Sam Sinclair breaking in, too, she has to decide just how far she's willing to go....

#289 RELENTLESS Jo Leigh
In Too Deep..., Bk. 1
Kate Rydell is living under the radar. When she witnesses a murder, the last people who can help her are the police, especially red-hot detective Vince Yarrow. But he's determined to protect Kate, even if he has to handcuff the sexy brunette to his bed....

#290 A SCENT OF SEDUCTION Colleen Collins
Lust Potion #9, Bk. 2
The competition for reader votes is heating up between journalists Coyote Sullivan and Kathryn Walters, and they're both determined to win. So what's going to give her the edge? A little dab of so-called lust potion and she'll seduce him out of the running!

www.eHarlequin.com